Taming Of The Brat: M/F Spanking Stories (Volume One) tells the tales of several naughty girls in need of a firm hand placed across their bottoms.

Past or present, some things never change…

… the mediaeval period during the Wars of the Roses, post Second World War, the '70s to today there are brats. What is a man to do when faced with a girl behaving in such a manner?

Taming Of The Brat answers that very question.

Whether in time of civil war, the coming home of a soldier to his beloved wife, summertime by the pool, in the workplace, an amusement park, the tennis locker-room or even at the beach. If there is a girl in dire need of a change in her attitude or behaviour, it is simple; there should be man who will not hesitate to put her over his knee and bare her bottom for a damn good spanking!

Taming of the brat?

… Taming of many brats.

Taming Of The Brat

M/F Spanking Stories
(Volume One)

R.S. Tanner

Taming Of The Brat: M/F Spanking Stories (Volume One)

Copyright © 2008 by R.S. Tanner

Published by Morgan Red

Photographer: Lev Dolgachov
Lev Dolgachov © Fotolia

Additional permission to use the images on the covers of this book has been granted by the photographer.

All rights reserved. No part of this book may be reproduced or transmitted in any form or by any means without written permission of the author.

ISBN: 978-0-9558529-0-9

It should not be presumed that either the model or photographer partakes or endorses any of the activities written in this book.

The author supports the freedom for consensual (or consenting to the sometimes non-consensual) spankings within a loving relationship or arrangement as much as he opposes corporal punishment upon the unwilling, outside of fiction, no matter their age.

"A dedication, if you please?"
"... Then, please. I will."

I dedicate this book to a very good spanko friend, little brat that you are, known in this book as *Kim*. Your honest feedback was much appreciated. You'll be happy to know that I am writing more relationship spanking stories; these will be the bulk of spanking stories to come... and yes, little one, you can rest assured that I will also include in future books some more of your specific fave relationship stories.

"I am R.S. Tanner… and I am a Spanko."

The individual desires for people within the spanking community vary. Such desires may stem from the same place or a similar experience. Finding a true connection between spankos, from the point of view from a vanilla, may seem simple. Of course, if you are spanko, it may become a little more complex.

'Why cannot things be simple?' a spanko might ask.

Indeed, and as Kim has pointed out to me, 'The world would be a much better place if it were full of spankos.'

It is a spanko's right to feel this way; I am sure that many spankos would agree.

However, if that were the case, you would not walk but a quarter of a mile without seeing someone bare bottom over another person's lap. Watching or being involved in the spanking, folk would not arrive at work on time, car crashes would occur through distractions, traffic jams all over the place because of spankings in the car or middle of the road.

Shall we ponder on what would happen within the work place? Picture this. 'If this deadline is not met there will be spankings.' Well, for the subs in this new spanking world, they would purposely fail to get themselves spanked. Moreover, the spanker may want them to, in order to spank.

Business men/women would not be concentrating, for example, on the stock market, but on the nearest bottom or on the lookout for the nearest hand. Not good.

People may spank instead of saying *shhh* in the cinema, thus causing more of a distraction due to people wanting to view the spanking rather than the film.

In short, it would be a disaster. Granted, this is the worst that could happen. After all, there are other things in life than spanking (oh dear, oh my... did I really say that?) Perhaps the number of spankos is best limited. Otherwise, the threat of a spanking in public would be meaningless.

A good thing though, war may not be so bloody. On the other hand (pun intended), it would not be good news for war films. Can we imagine the film *Troy* for example? Achilles and Hector fight, but not to the finish, they instead are trying to spank each other. No, no... not for me. Rather than the sacking of Troy, it would become the spanking of Troy.

In addition, let us say we have for the future two opposing armies, not bent on destroying one another; instead, bent on bending the enemy over their knee. In a total spanko world, everyone would join up. Well, only if the battlefield be a mix of males and females, depending on individual preference. Once again, this is the worst that could happen... or perhaps for the best (hmm).

Although now I think of it, same sex preference people have gay pride marches; why not have spanko pride marches... that is something I would pay to see.

As light-hearted an intro this section is, it all depends on the *top* treating the *bottom* in a way that suits them both. Sadly, there are those, and frankly too many people, whether from poor or rich nations, where being submissive is not a thing to joyously sing about.

Within a loving setting, be it an arrangement or in a relationship, spankings can, especially regarding the latter, bring two people closer together and ultimately, as it should be, they become happier.

This is, of course, common knowledge to those who are into such activities. To someone who is not into the scene, but is curious enough to read this or is a little interested and would like to explore it further, I would rather explain *my* spanko ways. This way no matter what other spankos may think, say or do, it does not reflect on the way that I am.

Not every spanko feels the same way towards spanking. How I feel, whether fun, role-play, sensual, sexual, maintenance, motivation or discipline spankings, they all have their own place and time. Such a time and place has often found itself debated; gradually as a society, we are improving our thoughts on spanking as discipline, i.e.: is not for the present day regarding children or the adult who finds it completely abhorrent. Of course, discipline is important within all our lives (not to sound like *Mr. Strickland* from *Back To The Future*... eep!), however, there are plenty of ways to apply such without corporal punishment, and I will use those as well.

Within a relationship or a bit of fun (lesser the case of the latter somewhat, if applying discipline, at least on principle), ranging from role-play to discipline as mentioned, spankings can play an important part. It seems to make it more special, more fulfilling and rewarding. It has a wonderful way of enriching the lives of those who are like-minded. I have no idea why, but for me, it is so.

I would not force a girl who was truly opposed to such ways upon her only to satisfy my own desires. That would not bring me any joy whatsoever.

If, for example, a girl disrespected me in a vanilla relationship, the ultimate threat would be to warn the girl to pack it in... or the relationship is over. Within a spanking relationship, I would say, 'Pack it in, right this second or you will find yourself over my knee!' If I needed to, I would be true to my word and make sure said brat learned her lesson.

If she would playfully mock or disrespect me, of course, that is a different matter entirely, though I may still provide such a girl's bottom with my firm and capable hand, playfully, of course... or perhaps a little harder.

Therefore, although things cannot be simple, everyone should realise, whether spanko (granted, already knowing so), vanilla or a nearly there/about to convert to becoming a/borderline-spanko that may glance through these pages, done the right way, along agreed upon consensual (or consenting to the sometimes non-consensual) spanking rules, spankings rule… and you know it!

Nevertheless, I shall return my focus to desires. Trying to please a variety of desires all the time may prove difficult. Some spankos prefer the *Daddy* dynamic whilst others prefer *Sir*, or perhaps any other chosen name. Speaking for myself, I am happy with both of what I have mentioned; it depends on the spankee.

The bulk of the stories I have written in this book (and for the future) involve a spanking relationship (Also known as, if implementing discipline, *Domestic Discipline*; otherwise known as, perhaps sounding a little better, *Adoring Discipline*) with a reference to the spanker as *Sir*; a few stories referring to the spanker as *Daddy*. From time to time, I will experiment outside of the husband/wife and boyfriend/girlfriend relationship theme (still remaining male top/female bottom), and hope they are, along with the heart of what I write, an enjoyable read.

Table of Contents

A Beach Brat
~Brat No. 1: Anna~..1
Daddy's Little Princess
~Brat No. 2: Kim~..25
Summertime By The Pool
(A late 1970's spanking story)
~Brat No. 3: Danielle – with Michelle and Claire~........47
Mediaeval Desires
(A Wars of the Roses spanking story)
~Brat No. 4: Christiana~..73
A Tennis Brat
~Brat No. 5: Jane – along with Hannah~...............123
A Soldier Returns
(A pre/post World War Two spanking story)
~Brat No. 6: Sarah~...149
Spanko Or Not A Spanko?
~Brat No. 7: Heather~..181

A Beach Brat
~Brat No. 1: Anna~

...*Run! Dammit run! Just keep running. Keep going... Run! Run! Run!*

Anna ran as if her life depended on it. She was in big trouble, and she knew it. She had not run in fear since childhood. That was when she had played a Halloween prank on a teacher...

Anna had found one of her teachers to be bossier than what was necessary, and although always fair with her, he was not regarding most of his pupils. She decided to exact some form of revenge.

Halloween was approaching. This provided the perfect opportunity to exact her revenge for the sake of others in disguise and do what she enjoyed most, which was behaving like a little brat without anyone labelling her a suspect.

The situation could have been worse, she thought. To

point out such, she even shouted words to that effect, including particular expletives that he would not appreciate. On reflection, this was not wise. Those words along with her reassurance, as expected, did not make him calm down. In fact, he became far angrier.

It was fun and exciting, and she knew it was wrong. This gave it extra appeal. Not to mention he could have actually caught her. One thing was certain; she did not want him to catch her!

This teacher had no idea it was she, and would never have guessed. As far as anyone knew, Anna was a good girl, a good student. Not so, though in part this was true. Anna was, indeed, a very intelligent girl. As such, her intelligence made it easy for her to scheme, be manipulative and ultimately get away with whatever she wanted.

As far as being a good girl. Let them think that. Haha!

She managed a lucky escape, cackling while she mocked him. Naturally, this teacher catching her was not an option she wanted to explore.

...**H**istory repeated itself with a difference. The situation was much worse; she was running from her husband. A wonderful man he was in so many ways, however, one thing that made him so wonderful involved an important part of their lives, was on occasions something she feared from him… spankings. In particular, the one that was due.

*

Anne -who preferred Anna- was a beautiful nineteen-year-old girl with a slim figure journeying to around five feet four inches; light reddish hair flowing passed her shoulders and green eyes shining so captivatingly. This gave her the advantage she needed in effortlessly manipulating men to either charm her way out of trouble or buy her what she needed. It was like a game. One in which she was very good at. Even so, there was more to it than simply batting eyelids. Finding a variety of ways without anyone suspecting she had any part in it was the challenge.

Anna had grown bored with such games. True, it was fun to have men buy her drinks all night without going to first base, yet managing to make them feel good about themselves. Clubbing was always an enjoyable way to practice her skills. She could additionally show off the latest fashion. It was not as if Anna was obsessed with the latest fashion, more she was able to obtain whatever the latest thing was without paying.

She wanted more from her relationships with men than this, but was unsure of what that was. Boyfriends would do anything to please her.

What girl wouldn't want that? Anna would muse.

She wanted much more. Someone that was able to challenge her. Anna knew damn well she was a spoiled little brat. She genuinely wanted to change, but had no ideas on how to undertake such a task. *Until that day,* she determined, *such behaviour will continue.*

During her break, she glanced through the financial newspaper, which was always among other newspapers on the staffroom coffee table. Although happy with her job, she was always interested in the job section that came with it once a week, to see whether a similar position was on offer with a greater wage. To her surprise, one such company was on the lookout for a new accountant that paid much more that her current employer for slightly less hours, stood out from any position she had seen advertised in weeks, besides the obvious stats as regards to pay and working hours.

Due to her intelligence, Anna was able to take the appropriate classes whilst still at school and became fully qualified.

Not surprisingly, she was also able to leave her employment on friendly terms.

Without hesitation, her resume was completed.

About a week and a half later, which was excessively long for Anna's impatient liking, she received a phone call informing her of an interview.

Shining as she always had in similar circumstances, surprise her it did not, that she had impressed her would-be boss, William.

She has a pleasant aura and is highly intelligent, he thought.

This was clear from her academic record, the reference from her previous employer, and from their conversation.

Anna's confidence in her ability to obtain any employment she desired made it easy to leave her previous employer. It was not a wise move, but she knew her previous employer would have her back in a heartbeat. As events turned out, the position was hers if she wanted it.

This annoyed her.

"Wanted it? What would be the point of applying if I didn't want the position?" Anna covered her mouth as soon as she had spoken. She could not believe those words had escaped her mouth. Perhaps, outside of her work, the boredom of her situation had made her more careless with how she presented herself. Perhaps the little brat within was escaping, which had been occurring more so of late. Part of her cared, but mostly figured the thought was not worth it, and so with that in mind, she removed her hand and returned to her upright positioned posture.

Strangely enough, a tingle of nervousness had crept inside Anna's stomach.

Surprised by such an outburst, William was shocked into

silence. It was certain that she was perfect for the position; at the same time, he did not like the attitude that suddenly released itself. She came across very cute when she quickly covered her mouth, and if he admitted it to himself, which he did, at that moment this girl was so damn adorable. Perhaps it was a mistake rather than a pattern of behaviour. Such occurrences were possible. Nonetheless, he would not allow it to go unnoticed.

William remained silent for a minute or so. He continued to maintain eye contact. Anna did not apologise, but was clearly beginning to look uncomfortable and unsure of the next few minutes.

Providing a thoughtful facial gesture and speaking gently, he spoke. "Hmm..." Changing from gentle to a more stern voice and countenance, he continued, "The position is yours. However, I will not tolerate such attitude. Had you been a man, I would not still be offering the position. I know accidents occur. This could well be one of them. I would strongly advise caution, little miss, and hope this will not happen again. Am I not in any way making myself clear?"

Anna sharply inhaled. It was her turn to be shocked. It was so long time since anyone had spoken so firmly to her. He had literally taken her breath away. She was happy that the position was hers, but confused with new feelings towards this man, her employer. *Think later*, she thought. For now, she needed to respond. "Y-yes Sir," she finally said, nervously, her head bowed a little.

What the hell was that! Stuttering. Head bowed. Oh, this cannot look good. She closed her eyes for a moment and slightly shook her head.

"Good girl." William smiled. He found his new employee ever so cute, *Even if it is a little on the bratty side.* This had its own appeal. He stood and walked towards her and offered his hand.

Anna stood, unsure of what to say. Finding it difficult to keep eye contact, she managed to shake his hand. "Thank you, sir. Sorry for..."

"Accepted. I am certain against any repeat. These things happen. If they happen again, I will need to be more firm with you." William directed Anna through the office until they reached the main door. "I look forward to working with you."

As they shook hands once more, Anna could only focus on William's comment about being more firm with her and his insistence that she call him by his first name. She knew men pretty well. It was clear he was attracted to her. In return, Anna appreciated his good looks and charm. He was tall with a shaved head and green eyes. Not many people had green eye, like her. It suited him well. In addition, she found his broad shoulders a highly attractive feature.

Over the following few months, William and Anna had gotten close; they began dating and shortly found themselves much more attracted to one another, and so began a serious relationship. Not much time would pass before she moved in with him.

During even the brief amount of time spent living together, William began to notice Anna's behaviour as she tried to manipulate him repeatedly. He wanted to put a stop to it before it got any worse.

Anna had not been feeling very well one week, and so William thought it best to wait until she was well again.

Arriving home from work and not wanting to disturb her in case she was asleep, he entered their home quietly.

To his great annoyance, William did not find his girlfriend asleep. He found her dancing around the living room to her favourite music. She had not noticed William until he turned off the television with the remote.

Anna wore only a blue t-shirt and tight white shorts. "I thought you'd be wrapped up better than that if you were truly unwell."

She went bright red at not only being caught dancing alone by surprise, but also her dishonesty had been uncovered. "I'm sorry."

"Sorry? You will be sorry, my girl. Now get here." He raised his voice and was very firm, which caught Anna of guard. She felt that she was in a little bit of trouble, but after all, what was the worse that could happen. He would not fire her. "You believe you can do whatever you want and get away with it, don't you?"

"Well, erm..." Anna said, pondering for a moment before answering. "Maybe... yes." *This was true,* she thought.

"I will change that. Now come here and bend over. You will do as you are told!"

Anna felt compelled to obey. She was pleased he was being firm with her. Those words had an unconscious part of her wanting to say, *Yes, sir.* Nobody, not even her parents had spoken to her in that manner. She knew what would happen. After all, unless William planned to have her bend over for sex, there was only one other thing he would do; his tone and choice of words had made it very clear as to his intentions. She could not bring herself to think of that word. Nevertheless, concerning that word, she felt William could do just that for taking control of her.

She bent over, legs together and held her ankles.

As she obeyed William's command, she felt an ever-increasing anxiety; increasing further as she wondered if he would actually go through with it.

Her attempts to breathe calmly were not successful.

William stood behind her and admired his girlfriend's

cute little bottom.

This is certainly long overdue for some firm discipline.

He peeled down Anna's shorts to reveal her bare bottom. "I see you did not want to wear any underwear today. It would not have mattered anyway. They would have been taken down as well."

Anna gasped much louder than she expected. "What..." Words failed to leave her mouth.

Her mind raced. *Oh, no! Oh, no! He really is. This is actually going to happen!*

The next few moments happened so quickly.

As a part of a sentence promising to try behaving, thus a way to avoid such discipline, she wanted to say, *What... wait a second!*

Before she had a chance, William had smacked her bottom hard.

"OOOWA!" Anna shouted, more exaggerated than out of pain. She knew why, but still asked, "What was that for!?"

Unknown to her, she did not feel a need to ask *what are you doing?* For some reason it felt natural that he would take down her shorts and spank her. She could now say that word in her thoughts... *spanking. I am actually getting one,* she thought. If she had been his daughter, it would have felt normal. There was a stronger feeling that it was normal coming from her boyfriend. It was what she had never received and always wanted, even if only on a subconscious level; she had not realised it until William's large hand smacked hard across her little bottom. *This is what I have needed for way too long.*

"You know what for, little girl," William scolded, answering her.

With those words, he stood her up, had taken hold of her arm and dragged her through his living room and into the kitchen. Her shorts had fallen to around her ankles.

She really felt like a naughty girl about to receive a spanking, but wondered, *I have needed this for so long. I want it. So why do I feel even more nervous now?!*

The realisation of her situation fast approached as she shuffled along, unable to speak. Even if she could talk, there was no chance of talking her way out of trouble.

He pulled out a chair from the kitchen table and sat. Anna was fixated on his lap. Time seemed to disappear in the moment he sat and lifted her. Nothing else mattered. Only her soon to be poor little bottom as William placed her over his knee. Now all she could view was the floor. Her bottom felt so exposed and she felt like a small child over what seemed like a huge lap. She felt so small.

In truth, Anna was. At five foot three and with William's height of six foot four, her feelings of being so small over this strongly built man's lap was well founded. All she had ever wanted and not realised until now was for a strong man not to hesitate in taking her over his knee, baring her bottom, and giving it a damn good spanking.

"Yeooow-Ow! Ow! Ow! Ow! Ow!" One thing was very clear. Anna did not have a high pain threshold as William's hand came down sharply across her bottom. Even though over his lap, each smack came as a strange surprise.

"I am not tolerating this, my girl." William got off to a good start in, as calm a manner as he could muster, firmly conveying the message that he was unhappy with her recent behaviour.

The sting that Anna felt was making such an impression very clear. She continued to yelp and cry out as his hand continued soundly smacking each cheek. "Sorry-Ow! Ow! Ow! Sorry, sir! Ow! Sorry! Ow! Ow! Ow!" she whined. *Jeez, does he ever take room to pause?! ...Owwww!* "Ow! Ow! Ow!"

He was taking her breath away. Literally, as Anna began to gasp for air.

When she caught her breath to speak, all the words that came out made her feel so much more like a little girl than what she felt already. Her loud cries of *Ow* and *Ouch* had changed into, for her, an embarrassing *Owie*, furthering her humiliation.

Although true, a spanking was what Anna had been craving without knowing and what was, she realised, needed as a regular part of her life was still humiliating. She was enjoying these new feelings and old yearnings finally answered, but at the same time seriously was not.

As a part of making a firm first impression, he only stopped spanking to scold his little brat of a girlfriend. "You have pushed me way too far, my girl, and I will not have it any longer. Some things need to be made clear."

"Yes, sir... Owie! Owie! Owie!" William's hand interrupted her agreeing words.

"I am not finished, my girl. Such things to make clear are, for example, if you ever dare speak to me disrespectfully or over spend, and although you haven't yet," William said, placing half a dozen more smacks across her bottom, "I will have you over my knee, just as you are now. The same goes for any bad behaviour including faking an illness to get away from work." The thought of her doing this angered him even more, and so he spanked even harder.

Anna could not take any more. Kicking and yelping out more desperately, she began pleading for forgiveness when newly formed tears began to form and fall from her eyes. Her face was still red from embarrassment at having her bottom smacked for the first time. Her bottom had already begun to match the colour of her face. She was pleased at how those tears brought along relief from the guilt of misbehaving.

William decided that the spanking would last for a few minutes more. After which, he would lovingly hold her.

With this spanking and each subsequent spanking Anna earned, an ever-increasing bond between her and William had formed.
Three years later, very happy and in love, they declared their commitment towards one another with the announcement of their engagement, and six months after this, they were married.
Anna had found the man she wanted. She especially enjoyed his strictness with her. It made her respect him even more. That, in addition with his love, had her feeling very much loved, safe, and secure. She did not want that to go away; William did not intend such to go away.

The weather had gradually turned to Anna's liking. She hated the cold, and when the weather was warm or hot enough for her liking, she enjoyed trips to the beach with William.

William, on the other hand, was not as keen on lazing around at the beach, but was happy to go along since it made his wife happy. When she was happy, it made him happy. Besides, it gave him a chance to catch up on his reading. He was not able to find the time to read as often as he would like. This proved an ideal time to do so.

It was a few months since they both had the time to enjoy a long day at the beach. Anna felt excited at being able to show off her new bikini that William bought her. She became over excited, which unfortunately lead to impatience.

"Come on. The sun will have gone down by the time you are ready," she whined, impatiently.

"Hey! You will sit your bottom down, right now, my

girl. I need to make sure we have enough..."

"Food," she said, abruptly cutting off her husband, "yes, I'm sure we have enough, even for you."

"Water," William sighed. He, too, was beginning to lose his patience. To prevent any thoughts in Anna's mind about misbehaving, he turned to face her and spoke in a low firm voice. "Keep up that attitude and we will not be going anywhere. You know very well, I mean it. Remember last time you pushed your luck at the beach. The day had ended much shorter than it should have. And when we arrived home, I gave you a damn good spanking. So, unless you want today to end the same way or end before it has even begun, I strongly suggest you behave yourself. Do I make myself clear?"

"Yes... sir." She sulked for the few minutes, having no choice other than to wait. Her mood changed when William had finished preparing the food, blankets, towels and such.

"Now, my little darling, we may leave. I'll let you open the door since I have my hands full. Just pick up that bag with my paper, book and sunscreen. Thank you."

They walked to their car, parked in the driveway. Anna, only wearing her bathing suit and sandals, was excited they were finally on their way. She loved to relax by the sea. There was a peacefulness she enjoyed, and equally if not more important, she could get a nice tan.

While William was putting the bags into the back of the car, Anna in her eagerness to begin the drive to the beach, with his keys in hand, sat in the driving seat, started the car and pressed the horn several times.

Frustrated, William quickly finished packing the bags into the back seat, closed the door and stormed over to the driver's side. Opening the door, and with a heavy hand, he smacked Anna across her thigh.

"Owwa!" Anna sharply glanced from left to right hoping

no one saw or heard. Fortunately, nobody was around.

Taking Anna by her hand, William yanked her out of the car, and scolded her. "You will get in the other side right now! Before I do something right here and now!"

There was no need to tell her twice. Anna moved at double her usual speed around the car, sat in the passenger side, and closed the door.

As soon as he sat in his side of the car and closed his side door, William shot a stern look towards Anna. This made her lower her head. "I told you to behave yourself. I did, did I not?"

Apologetically, still not wanting to make eye contact, she managed to let out, "Yes."

In a calmer manner, he said, "I know you are excited, my little darling, but I will still not accept any naughty behaviour from you." William reached out his hand and lifted her chin. "I do love you, little one," he said before kissing her forehead.

"Love you, too, sir."

Fortunately, the drive did not take long. The traffic was moderate. It could have been much worse, which pleased William. It would take forever to get there otherwise, not only due to the traffic in itself, but the domino effect of such. Anna would grow increasingly impatient with other people shortening her time at the beach. Ultimately, this would bring her to misbehave. To follow, a combination of traffic and misbehaviour from his wife would cause him much frustration. This would force him to pull over when he could find the right place and moment, and give Anna a damn good spanking.

In good time, they arrived near the beach.

Once parked, they got out of their car. William stretched and yawned out his tiredness. In contrast, so happy and full of energy, Anna seemed to bounce. The handprint that marked her thigh from when he smacked her had faded. It was barely noticeable. No one would have guessed that her husband had recently disciplined her for behaving like a naughty little girl.

Arriving early enough to rest at an area of their choice, they then, with William carrying most of what they needed, made their way onto the beach.

Once they had placed the hamper, blanket, towels, and other bags where Anna wanted, he put up the fence that would surround them, opening up towards the sea. This gave them a certain level of privacy.

William set up the sun chair in which he would spend most his time relaxed, reading unless he was lying next to Anna and petting her. She removed her sandals, searched through a bag, and found the sunscreen.

"Right. Now this is done." William sat on his sun chair, which had been leaned back so he could comfortably sit in and read. He removed his shoes and finally relaxed, happy to exchange a suit for a t-shirt and long shorts. He stood for a moment and looked around, and then sat on the blanket, upright with legs together out-stretched. "Lay across my lap, little girl."

"Huh? You can sit, kinda like, on my bottom to put the sunscreen on my back. Maybe even kneel beside me. Surely it hasn't been that long?" Anna asked, confused.

"I am aware, my little darling, but I am planning to do that in a minute." He placed his index finger on his right lap. "Across my knee. Now. Or we'll go home."

Knowing very well that William meant what he said, she whined, "I learned my lesson from when I was smacked in the car." Anna exaggerated the pleading look in her eyes.

Also knowing that he was firm with his decision by the look in *his* eyes, she stood for a moment and looked around. Thankfully, they were in an area not populated… yet. Since that could change at any moment, obediently, she knelt down, put the sunscreen on the blanket, and placed herself across her husband's lap.

Embarrassed and terrified at any one hearing... *Or worse, walking by and seeing! Please, no. Not that!* She buried her head in into the blanket. She rested her left hand just beyond her head and right hand to the right where, if needed, she could clench her fist, punch the blanket, and have that as an outlet for her pain. If she needed to scream, the blanket would be ideal to conceal it. That depended on how hard or long William intended the spanking to last.

William was going to make the spanking brief. He wanted it only as a reminder to behave. He peeled down her bikini panties.

Anna gasped, terrified... *Not my bare bottom!*

Speaking quietly, she begged, "Please, sir. Please, sir, make it quick." Her bare bottom on show, she hoped not on show to anyone other than her husband, especially in such a manner brought on humiliation. That alone, she thought, would be punishment enough.

William's hand came smacking down upon Anna's right bottom cheek, and then the left, alternating between cheeks. "I believe about twenty will be enough, for now, my little darling." Continuing the spanking, he scolded, "I also hope this will teach you to behave, and little girl, that I am not afraid to spank you outside." He liked how it sounded as his hand smacked across her little bottom in the open air.

"Ooooh! Owie! Owie! Yes. Yes, sir-Ow! It is. I will-Ow! Try, sir. Ow! Ow!" She tried to speak or cry out as softly as she could with the hope of no one else hearing. It was not easy since her little bottom had such a low pain threshold.

"I hope so. Otherwise I will give you another tanning, and it won't be the kind you want." He stopped at just over twenty smacks. "I'm finished. I hope you have learned your lesson."

"Yes, sir, I have."

"Good girl." William reached over for the sunscreen. Thinking she had permission to get up, she attempted to raise herself. "No, little girl, you will remain across my lap for the time being," he said, putting his hand on her back, forcing her down, across his lap again. "I will put this on your back, legs and bottom from here." He squeezed a generous amount onto his hand before putting the bottle beside him.

An appreciation for her behaving so naughtily was felt, not that he needed reminding, became reminded nonetheless, when looking upon her mildly pink bottom, appearing so damn cute.

Anna enjoyed the relief that the cream gave to her bottom. The spanking was not painful, but she did feel a little tingle; she was pleased with that. She could never take well a proper spanking. It was a warning well appreciated. Even more so considering it was in public. No one had seen or heard, but it could have easily happened. She most certainly *did not* want that.

William applied the sunscreen to other areas of Anna's body. It felt good for both of them as he gently massaged the cream into her soft skin. His hands spent a little more time petting her cute little cheeks with much enjoyment.

Feeling so relaxed, for several minutes she forgot that her little bottom was still on show to anyone who may pass by. The little fence erected around them helped keep their privacy, but not if someone happened to walk up to it directly.

It would be pointless for her to ask William to pull up her bikini panties. She knew how he would answer: *Only when I am finished,* followed by a smack. *And not a mo-*

ment sooner.

All Anna could do was lay across his lap and try not to worry. So comfortable was she that part of her did not care. If someone saw them, they would not know her or her husband, and they would only see his face. However, they would, perhaps, see William and her together, and put two and two together.

A few more minutes had passed.

Finally, she received a couple of taps to her bottom. Anna sighed with relief as he pulled back up her bikini panties.

"You may get up now, my little darling."

Anna got up and gave William a kiss. "Thank you, sir."

William put the appropriate amount of cream on his head, face, arms, and legs once Anna had finished covering other parts of her body with the sunscreen that he could not reach whilst she was across his lap.

"I am most likely to fall asleep, so don't forget to wake me, little one. I need to make an important business call. My phone needs charging, you see. I'll rely on you to set the alarm for two: thirty, if you could, please." William leaned back. Picking up the newspaper, he started reading.

"Okay, will do," she said, laying back on her sun chair, happy the sun factor level of her cream would protect her from burning, yet still provide a nice tan.

It was a pleasant and relaxing day. Work had been hectic over the previous month, and so for William it was the perfect day to forget about any business related thoughts. Well, almost. He needed to make a phone call regarding a high paying contract. If he did not contact the company in question around a certain time chances were it would go to someone else. The phone call would only last a minute, but was a very important minute.

After lunch, having read a little, William felt relaxed. He

fell asleep happy in the knowledge that Anna would wake him in time.

Anna turned over when the time was appropriate. The sun was shining and there was a peaceful atmosphere in the air. Although work had been hectic as of late, she did not bear the weight of responsibility that William held, but having a day to relax felt good. Any thoughts or worries could disappear. Apart from one thought. One in which had just entered her mind.

William slowly began to open his eyes. He yawned and gave his body a large stretch. That stretch felt just as pleasant as his brief sleep. It felt longer, but it was what he needed. He looked over at his wife and smiled. She appeared to look worried about something. "What's the time, little one?"

Anna sat upright and to the side of her sun chair. Her legs were close together with her hands gripping the edge along the side of the chair. "Um..." She dare say no more.

William suddenly realised why she was so worried. More firmly, he asked, "What is the time, little one?"

A very desperate tone shot out from Anna. "Look, I'm sorry. Um," she said, wincing, "nearly three: fifteen. I..."

"What..." he exclaimed, somewhat panicked, "didn't set your alarm. Yes, that is clear. I will be making myself clear in a minute, my girl!" He grabbed her phone and made the call.

Anna knew that what had been a very nice day so far was likely to end prematurely. It was also clear she was in for a damn good spanking when they got home. This additionally worried her. All that remained for her was to wait. The drive home would provide enough time to apologise repeatedly; she knew William would order her to be quiet. The result would be a lot of tears and a very sore bottom.

These thoughts were bouncing around in her mind whilst

William was apologetic on the phone about the lateness of the call. He provided some excuse. Anna could not hear the conversation, too preoccupied with her own thoughts. She could not control the butterfly feeling in her stomach.

William had finished the call; he placed the phone down under his chair. "You are a very lucky girl, little one. The contract is mine."

Anna sighed with relief.

"I would not feel so relieved if I were you, my girl. I am furious with you. Now come here." Expecting her to do as he commanded, William held out his hand.

"Excuse me?" Out of habit, she nearly obeyed. Suddenly she withdrew her hand. "No!" Anna appeared even more worried, and with good reason.

"You will do as you are told and come here, my girl." He grew increasingly angered with Anna as she shook her head. "Right, that's it. You're for it now!"

Just as William had nearly taken hold of Anna's hand, she quickly swung herself across her sun chair, got up, and ran.

Where to? Where to? she thought, desperately.

She had no idea as to where she could run to, only straight ahead, keeping her bottom that extra step out of reach of her husband's firm hand.

One thing she knew for certain was very clear... *A spanking, right there and then, was not an option,* she thought. Even if it were only one or two slaps across her bare bottom, for she knew he would pull down her bikini panties, at least one person would see or hear.

Panic had spread throughout her entire body and the butterfly feeling in her stomach increased. It increased even more, concerning both, when she glanced for a moment over her shoulder and saw William fast approaching.

William was clever enough to make it seem like a game.

If someone saw them coming, he would smile and make a comical comment to make it appear that they both were either having a race or were exercising.

Hearing him, Anna played along. She smiled, which was all she could do to make the situation appear everything it was not.

They were running for about ten minutes. Beginning to feel tired, Anna slowed down. Over a short distance, she was capable of outrunning William. Long distance, she had no chance at matching his stamina. A huge regret hung over her at not taking the opportunity to jog with him in the morning.

She shouted a swear word that began with the letter *f* at such a folly, and loud enough for him to hear. The way she figured it, he would spank her, and spank her hard. Swearing could hardly make it any worse, she hoped.

"I heard that, young lady!"

"You were meant to!" Anna turned to glance at him, not realising that whilst running, William had picked up a spade. He had not spanked her with a spade before. Perhaps aggravating him further was not such a good idea. She realised it would not be good news for her bottom to be spanked with such an implement.

Simple, but most effective... no doubt, she imagined with dread.

Run! Dammit run! Just keep running. Keep going... Run! Run! Run!

Anna ran as if her life depended on it. She was in big trouble, and she knew it. She had not run in fear since childhood. That was when she had played a Halloween prank on a teacher.

This particular memory flashed as if acted out before her very eyes. The parallels were not lost on her; they

were blatantly obvious. However, this time she knew it would end a lot differently.

Anna was nearly in tears, she was so exhausted. She could not keep going for much longer. Remembering a secluded area of sand dunes that would provide the ideal amount privacy, her feet headed in that direction.

Slowing down, and before she had a chance to think of what next she could do, she felt a sudden pull.

William had caught up with her.

Taking a firm grip of her arm, he proceeded to drag her towards the edge of a dune where it would be comfortable to sit. Anna had no intentions of protesting; she was far too tired for that. He threw the spade into the side of the dune so it stuck out, and then sat down and put his wife across his knee.

They both were regaining their breath, Anna more so. She knew it was pointless to struggle. It would only make her situation worse.

As soon as William gained control of his breathing, he began to scold his wife. "I hope you are well aware, my girl, of how close I came to losing that contract!"

He did not need a response from her. This was fortunate as she was too out of breath to respond anyway.

His hand began smacking hard across her bikini-covered bottom.

Anna desperately wanted to tell her husband how sorry she was, but still too out of breath to do so. All she could do was cry out in pain.

"I cannot believe how I could trust such a responsibility upon you... and you treat it in such a way." Unlike how he would usually discipline her, William was too furious to stop spanking whilst scolding her.

"You are in so much trouble for this, my girl!"

Regaining her breath became more difficult due to the force of William's hand landing across her bottom, thus taking the breath out of her no sooner had she gotten it back. She had no strength to move apart from breathing in and out, and that was not an easy task. Her bottom bounced with the force of each heavy thwack.

William paused for a moment to take down his wife's bikini panties. As he pulled them down, her tan lines made the centre part of her bottom look very sexy. It was almost white having turned a sunburn colour thanks to another kind of tanning.

Anna began to sob, more from actual remorse than of pain, which, at a steady pace, was increasing. She regained her breath enough to attempt an apology. "I'm really, really, Ah! Ow! Ow! Ow!" William was not interested in hearing how sorry she was just yet.

"You will be, my girl. Oh, by time I am done with you, you will be." The white area on her bottom not exposed to the sun was soon looking like it had been well and truly sun burnt.

Anna wanted to move, but fatigue had taken its toll on her. All she could do was lay sobbing across her husband's knee, and for a moment, yet again, forgot that she was across his knee out in the open, though for different reasons.

William stopped to take out the spade he had placed in the dune beside him.

Anna turned to look at what he was doing. "My G-Nooo! No, please!" Although her bottom had not received such an implement, she knew it would be painful.

Even with a touch of curiosity, his words were spoken firmly. "We will see if this has a desired effect, little one."

He held the plastic handle and allowed its hard plastic shovel end to find the answer.

Anna screamed out as a succession of semi-hard plastic

came whacking down upon her already sore little bottom. "I am glad I picked this thing up, my girl."

As the spade rained down, a tiny burst of energy from escaping deep from within her, she attempted to struggle. Wriggling in vain, her legs kicked up and down.

Her bottom continued to bounce.

Tears were steadily streaming down her face and her bottom was looking very much sun burnt at that point.

William finally stopped. "I believe you have learned your lesson, little one."

Anna sniffed. "Yes, sir. I have. I am sorry, sir." She could say no more as she continued to cry.

Throwing the spade to one side, William caressed her bottom. "You are very special to me, little one. Even as that is so, it will not save you from a spanking. But I do forgive you for your naughty behaviour." He ushered her to stand and still with her bikini panties down, sat her on his lap, leaned her into him, and gave her a good cuddle.

"Thank you, sir," Anna sobbed, crying into him. "Are we going home now?" she sniffed, cuddling into him.

"Only if you want to, little one, otherwise I am happy to stay an hour or two longer." William rubbed her bottom.

Anna had almost stopped sobbing. She flashed a smile at him. It disappeared when she realised, thinking aloud, "People are likely to see my spanked bottom. So we'll have to..."

"No we won't," William interrupted, thinking quickly. "We can walk back until we arrive near the crowded part. Then we can swim the rest of the way. When we arrive near to our spot, you will remain in the sea whilst I fetch a towel. You may then get out and run to me. I'll happily wrap you in it and give you a big hug. Then you can cuddle into me as we relax whilst I read for a while longer. You may fall asleep if you wish. If you are tired. After the swim, you will be. After a run and a spanking, I know you will be," he said, laughing. He knew his wife very well. "The towel still around you, no one will know."

"Okay. Thank you, sir." They both stood. Anna pulled down her husband and gave him a big kiss. "Love you, sir," she said, smiling as she pulled up her bikini panties.

She hugged into William as they began to walk back.

"Love you, too, little one. Even though you do things that are very naughty," he said, squeezing her. "You are a good girl, though. Don't ever change." Kissing the top of her head, he realised the contradicting sentence he just spoke, but Anna understood.

Anna said nothing as they walked along the shore, holding onto one another. She looked forward to cuddling into her husband when they arrive back at their spot on the beach. She did have a thought pertaining to what he had said… *As If!*

Daddy's Little Princess
~Brat No. 2: Kim~

If a person wanted to describe a girl named Kim, words such as cute, beautiful, sexy, bright, moody (at times), intelligent, fun, testing (again, at times), wonderful and adventurous would apply, and so much more; however, more appropriate are two words... little brat.

I am Ron, her boyfriend. Approaching five years, I have taken up the role that she had been craving for so long, her *Daddy*.

As such, a part of her wants and needs, of high importance are plenty of cuddles and petting. There is one other aspect superseding even these two, aside from my English accent, which to her American ears was adored; on occasions when in a bratty mood, she might playfully mock (a decision that could possibly put her little bottom in an awful lot of trouble).

In return, I found her accent ever so adorable, especially

when she had been naughty and was due for the inevitable. The inevitable that I speak of happens to be the aspect of high importance to her; when needed or desired, done in the right way, which I do, is a good smacked bottom.

Spankings were not apart of Kim's life growing up, but she loved the world of spanking, whether she saw it in films or comics. As she grew and those desires increased, she loved it when men would talk to her in a firm manner. If they threatened a spanking, her heart would beat fast; if she was on a date and they decided she needed a trip across their knee, this was answering her innermost desires.

There was a slight draw back to this. Many men would enjoy taking her across their knee, but unfortunately, this little girl wanted the atmosphere to be right for her; only one man seemed to know how to do this properly.

I am very happy that she behaves in a manner that would earn her a spanking. I would not want it any other way. Plenty of times her bratty behaviour is cute, but still warrants my hand being put across her bottom, if only mildly.

There are times, when I am a little short of my usual patience and she is pushing me as much as possible, I feel I could yank down her pants and panties in one sudden motion, and give a swift smack to her bottom in public. One flaw in this is that people are unlikely to shrug off such a thing in a modern society.

Such a desire provides both an element of excitement or deterrent. The deterrent is that she knows her Daddy will, if pushed too far, smack her bottom in public; she does not want the embarrassment of any one witnessing a little girl receiving such. To be embarrassed in front of her Daddy... yes. Embarrassed in front of others... no. As tempting a thought it may be to her; a fantasy to fulfil in front of spankos and non-spankos alike. The latter is a dare she would push as far as she could, but when reality sinks in, a little girl would fast realise another place she would rather be.

I have given a swift smack, but light in comparison to that in which I would prefer, as a warning for her to behave, and only delivered when no one is likely to have seen.

Disciplinary spankings are sometimes, or more accurate, often warranted. Kim would disagree, often reminding me, "I am perfect. I'm a princess."

I would reply, "Even a so-called perfect princess needs her Daddy's hand put across her little bottom, and very hard, indeed, if she is too naughty."

Kim would respond with a typical, "Hmph!"

Today, I had woken up early. For the moment, thoughts wandered across my mind as I watched her sleep. Unbeknownst to her, Kim did appear as the image of an angel that she had many a time claim herself to be, most often when naughty. Nevertheless, the picture of a cute angelic little princess was fast asleep.

My little one often favoured sleeping naked, but since this night had been cold, she wore her nightie. In blissful contrast, under the blanket, the atmosphere was very cosy.

While I gazed at my little girl, the mere thought of her made me want to speak of her as if straight from a modern Shakespearian play.

My large hand caressed along her body as she lay on her side, leaning towards her front, and away from me; as if ready for the romantic connection of two spoons. My hand flowed gently in the direction towards her bottom. Curving like a resplendent mountain made by Venus' own hand, and heaven to the fingers of such a male hand that have privilege and pleasure to wander across. The cotton material had its own amazing charm, for it was this layer that covered her skin, enticing my hand further to gaze upon her barest form. Such a sight if any a man had seen of beauty in its natural form.

With slow and gentle intent, I peeled her nightie backwards and revealed her cute little bottom. I could not have the pleasure of viewing such a wondrous sight for the moment, but know of its radiant allure. Like a blind man creating an image in his mind whilst slowly moving his fingers over an object, I, too, would move my fingers across such an object of desire, though of course, she was more than just an object of desire.

Kim had a small bottom, well shaped and full bodied that made it ideal for a spanking. By design it rendered itself perfect for (indeed, begged and cried out for) a firm hand to smack hard across such delicate skin with the ability to absorb such punishment. Its accompanying purpose was for the lighter touch of caress from either hand or lips. For no lips could grace such a surface of perfection.

For the moment, my hand explored the area of her beautiful smooth bottom. Gliding from one cheek to the next, across the middle where the cheeks separated, and around its sides, and back again. My hand ventured towards her upper thighs where my hand would yearn to caress her bottom, and so retreat once more. My mind wandered to a few of so many times that warranted a need for a little girl to have her bottom bared.

Such of the many, many times my little girl would be in need of having her bottom bared was when she behaved like a little brat; either comical or to a stage where it became clear a disciplinary spanking was called for, and as to be expected, occasions where it would be a little of both.

****

One night we were lying in bed, cuddling before turning over and going to sleep. As our conversation ended about our day, my little girl, as cute as ever, was making fun of me as the topic of *Shrek* and ogres came about.

"Has anyone called you that before?" my little girl asked, referring to Ogres; she had a suspiciously inquisitive, naughty look upon her face.

"Er... no," I answered with curiosity, remaining suspicious throughout.

With an ever so deadpan manner, my little princess then enquired, "What about all those people that cross over your bridge?"

My mouth opened wide. I was not expecting such a response. It was very funny, and although on principle I should not have, I could not help but laugh along with my little girl, already cheekily doing so. Almost as soon as I finished laughing, I smacked Kim's bottom.

Throwing the bed covers away from us, I got up and lifted my little girl. Kim was ready to fall asleep; not necessarily in the mood for a spanking, she was happy to receive my hand across her bottom a few times before bed.

She accepted the inevitability of her situation as I sat and put her across my lap. Looking as cute as ever, wearing no nightclothes, only her wonderful smooth skin and her long blonde hair, flowing across her back; standing out most of all was such was an even more beautiful bare bottom. It would not be long before that bottom made the transition from a pale white to a (much more pleasing to the eye) shade of pink.

I caressed her bottom and told her, "Although it was highly cute and very funny, behaving like that will result in a little girl's bare bottom pointing in the air, across her Daddy's knee about to be spanked."

The spanking was only mild. After all, it was only a bit of fun; my approach was mock-serious. Even so, I found it my utmost *Daddy duty* to make sure my hand delivered a sting to my princess' little bottom, all on principle, of course.

****

This particular time, Kim was incessantly pushing her luck. It was cute at first, but in due course, her actions would culminate in a Daddy tolerating it no longer.

There was only one way to correct such unwanted behaviour; she was in dire need for me to be firm and take her in hand.

"**B**end over my knee," I scolded, sitting on the bed.

A familiar phrase within our lives, Kim knew it was in her best interest to obey, and often would. This particular time she was a little drunk. I would not allow her to drink too much considering we had to wake up early the next day, but enough to be merry. As a result, it made her more determined to be defiant; the wine had made her a little more brave than usual.

It was around one o'clock in the morning. As we had just finished watching a film, I decided that we should get ready for bed since we had arranged to get up early the next day. Our plans were to spend as much time as we could at our favourite theme park. To enjoy most of our time there, we would need to wake up early. Staying awake any later was something I could not allow.

Kim, by the look on her face, had other ideas. I was certainly not allowing her to have her own way. Scolding more firmly, I told her, "You will move your little bottom here, right now."

After folding her arms, she sank deeper into the sofa. Not wanting to listen, she shook her head and with a pout, had dared to say, "No."

"Excuse me. What was that, little girl? You will shift your bottom here and bend over my knee. If you do not, we will not be going tomorrow. And you will still be spanked."

"Nah-Uh," Kim said in a low tone. Deep down wanting a spanking, but she also knew we would be going to the theme park anyway. She was in no mood to willingly place herself over her Daddy's lap.

I stood and looked down at her. She remained seated not more than half a dozen paces away. I responded in a typical stern but gentle condescending manner. "Uh-Huh."

"Nah-Uh!" This time an even more determined brat emerged.

"Uh-Huh, little girl," I said in a more stern voice.

"Pft."

"That's it." I walked towards my little girl who, giving a little giggle, found something amusing. I decided there was a need to change that.

She new a spanking was in her future, but was still determined not to go easily; she weighted herself down all she could when I took hold of her. Kim squirmed with a smile combined with her bratty countenance. It was as if she wanted to test if I was man enough to tame her. There was never any doubt as to whether or not I was.

She did not enjoy having her legs smacked, so I gave a hard whack across the side of her thigh. As she shot a brat filled glare towards me, the momentary distraction provided enough time to lift her and carry her to our bed. I placed her down for her to only run off, giggling as she jumped onto the sofa.

I began to lose my patience. "That does it! Do you want me to take off my belt?"

Kim gasped. "No! You wouldn't. I'm a princess."

"Yes, I would, little girl. I have done so before and I will do so again."

"Pft! I'm not scared." To prove my little girl I was serious, I began to loosen my belt.

The belt was an implement that would catch her attention immediately. Kim would not freely admit it if she was scared, but the threat of its use made her more obedient. She knew how even when used lightly it would create a sting she would wish to avoid.

"Grr... fine!" she relented. Once I had removed my belt, Kim decided to take it off me and throw it to the far side of the room.

"If I think you're in need of it, little girl, I'll just go find it. Now bend over my knee." I would not need its use. It was getting late, so a brief and well-felt spanking would suffice.

I sat in the middle at the end of our bed. Kim approached and gently placed herself comfortably across my lap.

I caressed her bottom whilst I scolded. "You have been a very naughty little girl."

"Nah-Uh!" she protested.

I gave a hard smack across the middle of her bottom.

"Ow!" she said quietly, sounding adorable.

"Right, little one. Before I spank, you will answer a few things for me." On occasions, either before a spanking or as a warning, I would ask a set of ritualistic questions.

"What happens to a little girl that doesn't know how to behave?" I asked.

"She gets spanked," my little girl answered, slowly.

"Good girl. And how does she get spanked?"

"On her bare bottom."

"And how?"

"Over the knee."

"Who does the spanking, little one?"

"Her Daddy."

"Good girl." I patted my princess' little bottom and prepared my hand for aim.

Kim had questions of her own for me. If not answered, she would brat even more. "What are you spanking me for?"

My hand came down hard upon her bottom with a steady pace, but not too fast. "You are being spanked, little girl, because you refused to go to bed, for one."

It was highly pleasurable spanking such a cute bottom, but I was not going to make that more obvious than the fact that I am a spanko. I was not pleased, on principle at least, with my little girl's behaviour.

My hand smacked each cheek, alternating the pattern, so Kim could not predict when my hand would land.

"Secondly..." I paused the spanking for a moment.

"Ha! You don't even know what you're spanking me for-Ow! Ooh! Ow! Ow!"

"Oh..." I reassured her, smacking a little harder, "yes, I do, little one." Kim's bottom could take a hard spanking, and so there was a fleeting need to remove any form of protection. In addition, with such cheek, it would not be long before her bare bottom felt my hand.

"Right," I said, deciding to caress Kim's bottom for a moment. "This is clearly not spanked enough." My hand rained down on her bottom, as she deserved. "Secondly, you are being spanked for wanting to drink even more, knowing full well we need to get up early tomorrow."

"Ow, Ow, Ow... Fine! Ah! Ow! Ow!" Kim rested across my lap and waited for her bottom to become bare, for she knew well enough, it was only a matter of time.

I peeled down her panties and revealed my princess' cute little bottom. "Before I continue, I will give a kiss for luck. You'll soon need it." I gently kissed each cheek twice, one at each top and bottom area. Wanting to catch her off guard, I did not inhale as I raised my hand.

"Owww!" Catching my little girl off guard had the desired effect. I proceeded by returning to a steady pace making sure my little girl felt every smack.

"You need to learn, little girl, that when your Daddy tells you that you need to go to bed, you listen, and then do as you are told," I scolded, noticing my little princess' legs rising. "Lower your legs, right this second, my girl." I pushed them back down.

Kim's bottom rippled as my hand made it bounce. "Ah! Ah! Ow! Ow! Okay-Ow! Ow! Okay." Normally my little girl could take a very hard spanking but with one drawback. She bruised easily. She was feeling the effect of my hand, more so being drunk, which came to me as a surprise. "My butt's gonna fall off!" she said, sounding ever so cute.

"Don't be silly," I said, slowing down my pace. "I know you bruise easily. That's another reason to spank. Eat more fruit. More *vitamin C* would help prevent that."

"Bah!"

I spanked even harder for a moment. "I beg your pardon, little girl!"

"Ow! Ow! Yes, Daddy."

"That's better. You know I will give you plenty of aftercare, so don't be silly. Apologise, and I will stop."

This is something Kim did not enjoy doing, defiantly saying, "Mean!-Ow! Ow! Ow!"

"I am firm but fair, little girl." My little girl's bottom had turned a satisfying red. I could feel how heated it became.

"Ow! Ow! Stop! Ow! Ah! Okay, Okay, Fine! Sorry!"

"Without the attitude, my girl," I said, smacking a little harder. "And sorry, what, little girl?"

"I said I'm Sor-Ow! Ow! Ow! Ooh! Ooh! Okay-Ow! Sorry, Daddy!-Ow! Ow!"

I stopped and caressed my little girl's stinging bottom. It was breathtaking to gaze upon and feel such a transformation; pale white and slightly cold to a reddened and heated little bottom... very warm and cosy.

"Right, young lady," I said, raising her off my lap, "you will come with me." I led her to the corner with her pants and panties still around her ankles. "You will stay right there."

"Corner time is so lame," my little princess protested.

"It serves a purpose, and that is for you to reflect on your naughty behaviour." As I walked away, she attempted to pull up her panties. "No, little girl, you will do corner time bare bottomed." I pulled her panties down again.

The moment I walked away, she attempted to walk away from the corner.

"Don't you..." I scolded firmly... as in *Don't you dare!* Of course, I believe she knew the sentence I had no need to finish. She giggled as my hand gently pushed her back into the corner. "You will stay right there." I smacked her bottom half a dozen times. "Or I'll put you over my knee again, little girl." She had not expected to receive my hand at that time, and with her low sounding *ow's*, she sounded so cute. Her cuteness enhanced as she slowly rubbed her bottom. "Right. I'll be back in a second." I moved towards the drawer.

"Where are you going?" she asked.

"I'm gonna get that cream."

"Well, hurry up," she told me, impatiently.

"You..." There was no need to add *little brat*. Again, she already knew the ending to such a sentence uncompleted. I walked over towards her and smacked her bottom a further four more times; this time she had expected my hand. "Do not!"

I picked up the cream that was on the drawer, thinking

again how adorable my little girl looked, as she stood with her spanked bare bottom. I sat down on the bed. "Come on, little one. Over my knee."

Happy that her bare bottom corner time was over, my little girl obeyed without a fuss. She also loved to receive the after-care. As always, I found it a pleasure to apply the cream to her sore little bottom.

After I had sensually applied a generous amount of cream, I kissed each cheek. "It's time for bed, little girl."

"Yes, Daddy," she said, sounding tired.

We got undressed for bed.

Once in bed, I gave her a little cuddle and kissed her forehead before we turned over and went to sleep.

The next day was very hot. This did not help improve my little girl's mood. She was behaving well enough for the moment, but I could sense that this would not last long; not having the amount of sleep a little brat would have preferred.

On our way to the theme park, I ate just over half a tub of mixed fruit, which I had bought the previous day; with the plastic fork, I fed my little girl while she drove. Eating a little helped her mood somewhat.

When we arrived, I took a photo with my phone of the parking zone. It would later come in handy when there was a hurried need to return to the car.

We had a little something to eat before going on any rides. This improved my little girl's mood some more, but the lines were long for most rides, and that did not help keep either of our moods heading in the right direction. Normally we would choose a quieter day and not have to wait long at all, if that, and so would make the day more fun.

It was not entirely her fault. It was in her nature to become bratty or moody if stuck in a line for too long. I had more patience, but even I was growing frustrated. We tried to not let it ruin the day. However, a couple of hours into our time at the park, I was not going to tolerate any attitude directed at me.

"Unless you want a spanking, I would change that attitude." Considerately, I scolded quietly, aware people may hear.

Kim sharply looked around, annoyed that anyone may have heard. "Not too loud."

"No one heard, but keep it up, Kim, and they will hear a lot more."

As we approached the rest rooms, giving out a frustrated groan, she walked into the Ladies. I let out a massive sigh of my own, pulling down on my face as I looked to the sky. I entered the Gents side. When I was finished, I knew a much-needed talk was fast approaching with my little girl.

Whilst I waited for a minute more, I noticed, for a change, how few in number there were people in this area. I decided to take advantage of this. The entrance to the Ladies and Gents had a wall that led to them. This was perfect for what I intended.

When my little girl came out, she enquired, "Okay, where to next?"

"First off, how many people were in there?"

"Um, none. Which is kinda weird." Once that realisation had passed, her countenance grew to that of impatience; wondering the entire point of this conversation.

"Good. Then no one will see this." With a solid smack my hand whacked across her little bottom. Kim tried to say something, but before she had a chance, I had firmly taken hold of her arm. "I will not be having your attitude any longer. I am surprised I have allowed it so far. You will pack it in and behave yourself, little girl, or I will take down your pants and spank you right now!"

"No!" She was certain of that.

"Excuse me?" As I saw the situation, my little girl was in no position to argue about whether or not she would have her bottom smacked.

More annoyance began to surface from Kim as her moodiness cemented. "I'm not in the mood!"

With a firm look in my eyes, and emphasising each word slowly, I said, "Neither am I!"

"Pfft!" Kim waved her hand not caring about the mood of anyone other that herself.

As she looked up, tired of talking, I had taken her pants and was about to thrust them down when the realisation of what I was about to do had dawned upon her.

Shocked and with mouth open, Kim tried to say something, but was suffering from temporal paralyses of the mouth. Her eyes were as wide as I had ever seen them. She quickly looked down and held a firm grip on her pants to enable them to remain exactly where she wanted. My princess' eyes, with a look that changed from shock and disbelief to growing anger at the thought of a possible spanking in public (especially one that could well have been on her bare bottom), focused next on me.

Kim's voice was in the process of returning to her when I took her arm and began walking, speaking quietly as people began entering the area. "You are in big trouble, little girl. It would be in your best interest to take my hand willingly."

She was far from happy with this, but knew that I would drag her, thus creating a scene that would hardly go unnoticed; a scene she did not want to act out.

"Fine!" Grudgingly, she held my hand.

Even though about to be spanked, just as she did not want others to see herself dragged, she did not want others knowing she had just had a fall out, of sorts, with her boyfriend.

The silence as we walked through the theme park gave Kim plenty of time to think. Any other time, knowing how badly she behaved, she would have realised that she needed a spanking. That time had not yet arrived.

A nervous feeling grew within her. My little girl knew I would discipline her in the only place that could provide a touch of privacy. That would be her car.

"At least I can drive," she muttered.

"Don't even, little girl," I quietly scolded.

The fact that my little girl could drive and not I, gave her a sense of superiority at this point, while we waited for the long transport train to take us back to the car park.

"Are you ready to say something?" I queried. Kim's anger had subsided, but her moodiness had changed into a more brattified version combined with stubbornness. "Oh, you are not helping yourself."

"Bah!"

"Again, little one..." I emphasised each following word, "not helping." My own anger had subsided at this point, and found it cute and a little amusing at my little girl's brattiness. I would not tell her this at that point. "Ah, here it is. Come along, little one."

"Well, obviously!" Okay, the humour of her behaviour faded somewhat with this snotty comment. If not for the fact that I was feeling self-conscious about spanking her blatantly in public, my hand would have whacked very hard across her backside (on reflection, perhaps I should have delivered a one-off smack).

As we sat in the transport train we let go of each other's hand. Kim's body language could not have been clearer, even if she had waved a placard above her head.

If we were in a cartoon, a *thought bubble* would have appeared. It would have said something like this: Grrr... -

Bad language that would earn a severe smacked bottom- ... -Again, bad language that would earn a severe smacked bottom- ... Grrr... I'm a PRINCESS... Princesses DON'T get SPANKED unless THEY WANT IT! ... Bah! ... Pfft! ... Ogre! Ogre! ... -More bad language that would earn a spanking- ... Fat Ogre!

She was almost out of the transport train; turning her body that much away from me. When she looked at me for a moment, I chose to clench my jaw and shoot a highly displeased look that stated how cross I was with her. If my little girl could not have guessed by this time, my eyes told her that she was in big trouble. Knowing full well how hard it would be for her to sit on those rides if I allowed us to return to the park, a moody little girl altered her body language and gulped.

Once the transport train had stopped, we got out; I took hold of her hand once more. As we walked towards the parking area, I briefly looked at my phone and searched through the pictures to find the zone where we had parked. My little girl can walk fast when wanting to go on particular rides, but I had surprised her at how fast I can walk when I felt there was a need. Her legs were shorter than mine being that I stand about nine or ten inches taller. I made her break into a little trot to keep up with my pace.

Our car was in sight when my little girl tried to persuade me, "What if people see?" she asked, her nervousness steadily increasing.

"Then people will see a Daddy spanking his little girl." I had considered such a possibility. "Open the back door, little one. Thank you." Under the back part of the front seat, just for such an occasion, I had put several window tints that I could place against the window (easily removed as and when needed), and therefore provide us with the privacy we desired.

As I began placing them on the window, I informed my little princess, "I was not able to buy as many as these as I wanted. Will have to buy some more later."

"Wait a sec. You're not putting those up," she protested.

"Do you want others to see you being spanked?" At that moment, I did not worry about anyone overhearing what I had said. My princess' reaction was somewhat different; she shot her head around to see if anyone heard. "I didn't think so. If we put them in back parts of the car that should be enough privacy. What are not covered be the windows to the front of the car, the drivers side, and the shotgun side." After I had attached the last tint to the side of the window where I would enter the car, I sat in the back, and ushered my little girl to do the same. "If someone looks in from there," I said, pointing to the front, "they will see you getting exactly what has been coming to you."

"What if someone..."

I interrupted and took hold of my little girl's waist and put her across my lap, my hand smacking hard against her bottom. I made sure she was comfortable as I was. Wearing her beige pants, she almost looked bare bottom from a distance. I was not in any mood to spank from pants to panties, and then on the bare; I exposed my little girl's bottom as soon as possible. Her pants were jeans-like material and more difficult to take down than sports pants, either one looked very sexy on her.

I had pondered whether this was the reason she thought she could get away with such behaviour. "Other men may be happy to tolerate this behaviour, my girl!" I scolded, tugging down her pants, "but *I* will not." I pulled down her panties causing my little girl to gasp as her bare bottom was on show to the world. Well, the world that could see the middle level of the car parking area through the rectangular windowless-like gap as our car parked against the wall.

"Ow! Ow! Ah! Ooh! Ah! Ow!" My little girl's bottom was still tender from the spanking the night before. She blushed as she could hear the sounds of cars driving passed. We could see out well enough and if all worked to plan, nobody would be able to glance in and see what we were doing (or, if more accurate, what I was doing to my little girl). That is, of course, *if* the plan worked.

"You have pushed me way too far, my girl." As my hand continued smacking hard across my princess' little bottom, those cheeks began to blush as well. "This attitude will come to an end. I don't know why you thought I'd allow it to continue. Did you think I wouldn't take you back to the car?" I must admit, it did feel a little strange. Almost as if people could actually see what I was doing. If there was a chance anyone could see or hear, they did not outwardly show signs of knowing.

"Oww! Ow! Owie! Owie! No-Ow! Ow! Sorry, Daddy-Ow! Ow!"

"Don't you even think that by quickly saying *sorry, Daddy* it would make me stop." I began to spank faster, which made my little princess squeal louder. "I would hope you are a sorry little girl."

I stopped for a moment. My little girl attempted to get up, only to receive a hard whack across her increasingly sore little bottom. "Owwie! What?" she asked, confused, "what Daddy? What's up?" She looked up, and gasped, "Oh, God!" She quickly then buried her head.

"They cannot see, little one." I wondered as I watched a car park next to us. Curiosity being what it is along and human nature, a group of older teens that had exited their car, two of the group began to look closer at the tinted window. "They are beginning to look closer. Anyway," I said, confidently, dismissing any worrying thoughts.

"Nooo!" my little girl protested, ever so quietly. "They

could still hear."

I caressed her bottom for a moment, and then spoke. "Then they will hear a Daddy spanking his little girl. Now you be silent." I could feel my heart beating faster, too, but still needed to finish disciplining my little princess.

Fortunately, in the next few moments, I heard one of the group call out, "Are you coming or not?" They both then ran off to catch up.

I wanted my little girl to feel as panicked as she was for those few minutes, a minute or so more. "There or not, I am finishing this."

"Nooo!" my princess squealed, and much louder than she had expected. She buried her head as much as possible, in dread of others seeing her in such an exposed and vulnerable position.

To finish off, I spanked extremely hard, making my little girl cry out very loud as I scolded firmly. "You will never act like that towards me in public, my girl. You even so much as dare give me a little attitude and your bare behind is in serious trouble, no matter who may see! Do I make myself clear?!"

"Owie! Owie! Owie! Ow-Owwww!!" she began to sob, much out of the thought of others seeing and hearing her as well as the pain. "Yes-Ow! Ow! Ow! Yes Daddy-Ow! Ah! Ah! Oww! Yes, Daddy!" she sniffed.

I stopped and began caressing my princess' stinging and very sore little bottom. "I believe you have learned your lesson."

"Yes. I mean… yes, Daddy," she said, in a quiet manner and sniffing again.

"That group had walked away, you know," I said, softly informing her. "I wanted you to think they may have seen or heard as an extra punishment."

It seemed as if my little girl had sworn under her breath.

I began smacking her bottom once again and very hard. "I beg your pardon, little girl! You do not use language like that. No little girl should and I will not allow it to go unpunished." I stopped to allow an apology.

"Oww! Ow! Ow! Ow! Owie! Owie!" She began to cry louder. "Sorry, Daddy!"

I caressed her bottom again. "Good girl. Unfortunately for you, I don't have any cream on me."

"I do," a little girl informed me, sobbing.

I leaned over and saw the bag in question on the floor. I picked it up by the handle, placed it on her back, and searched through. "Ah yes, here it is. I'm not sure you deserve this for your behaviour, princess." I contemplated for no more than a second or two, but waited a little bit longer.

"Please, Daddy!" she pleaded, sobbing away.

I removed the lid and put a generous amount of cream on my hands and my little girl's bottom. I began to rub it in; she moaned loudly with relief. I could view another private area and saw how wet it was. A punishment is was, and true, it stung, but still, a good smacked bottom was a turn on for her. It was a turn on for me, too, which she could most likely feel.

Before we would carry on and enjoy the remainder of our day (without a doubt, the spanking had not only cleared the air, but also brought us closer together), in the car, we would enjoy a good cuddle. But before even that and before something else, for several minutes, we both enjoyed my large hands relieve a remorseful little girl's stinging and sore bottom.

****

Although disciplinary spankings occurred, they were not typical at our favoured theme park; a fun type of spanking was more likely. That is, whenever possible…

One day (a very good day) as the park was closing, my little girl would find herself on the receiving end of a fun type of spanking, bare bottomed and across her Daddy's knee, whilst on our favourite ride.

The day was nearing an end, and as one by one, the rides were closing, people were leaving the park. We had fortunately timed it just right so that we were the last two for a certain ride.

It was a ride that was both relaxing and enjoyable. Without a doubt, the perfect way to end the day, and even more so if we could get away with what we had planned.

The thought of such a plan, alone, was exciting; as we were deciding the right moment, Kim had nearly let her nerves get the better of her. I reassured her that everything would go as planned, even though I had no idea whether it would or not.

Surely, I thought at the time, they would have security cameras likewise with the park, throughout the ride. All we could do was hope that since it was the end of the day, all that the staff wanted was to go home, and so nobody would be paying much attention to the ride itself.

Since the ride was dark, this boosted (perhaps wrongly so) our confidence; we waited for the right moment to approach when it was at its blackest. I could not spank as hard as either my little girl or I would have preferred, but even a tap would be enough to satisfy us both. It would not last long either, but having the nerve to do so would more than make up for that.

As I ushered her across my lap, I was expecting a loud voice to echo through the ride telling us to remain properly seated like when someone had reached out his or her arm to touch something along the way.

That ride appeared in a whole new light as my heart, and the heart of my little princess', raced with excitement.

Once across my lap, the next task was to bare my little girl's bottom. As I peeled down her pants and panties, I cannot remember such pleasure at viewing her beautiful bottom. If anyone happened to glance at the security cameras at that point, they would have seen a very cute little girl, bare bottomed and across the lap of a highly fine looking fellow (if I do say so myself) about to be spanked.

I gave her little bottom a few very light smacks before allowing her to return seated, shuffling up her pants and panties as she did. The smile on her face told me she enjoyed her brief time across my lap as much as I, and although already our favourite ride, we took even greater pleasure, a Daddy's arm around his little princess, in relaxing as we sailed through the remainder of the ride.

When the ride had finished, since there were no strange looks from any of the staff, I can only assume that what we had done (until now, that is) went unknown.

In any case, it certainly was the best way to end what had been a very enjoyable day... a day that (although soon enough would technically be so) was not yet over; before bed, and pleasurably so, my special little girl would receive my hand more firmly across her bottom than was, of course, possible on the ride.

Summertime By The Pool
(A late 1970's spanking story)
~Brat No. 3: Danielle – with Michelle and Claire~

It was a hot 1977 summer day, and Drew was being as patient as he could with the girls. They were acting in a very loud manner, amongst themselves and with their music, which he enjoyed, but not that loud on a hot day. He was a liberal person, but this time was different; three girls, and one in particular, had him thinking about doing something that was very much out of character. They had all pushed him beyond his usual tolerance with their obnoxious behaviour over the past week, flouting almost every rule he game them.

The girls were living in his home for a minimal cost, just a little amount to cover part of the expense for the additional food needed. One of the three girls, he mentored; Michelle aged twenty. Her two friends were Danielle and Claire, both nineteen. They were college students, which over the past two summers, Drew allowed to stay with him since he lived closer to the centre of town. None of the girls could drive, so this gave them more of a chance to enjoy their time off school.

All three had a similar cute look and could easily pass for sisters. They had known each other since junior high school and had been best friends ever since.

They all had blue eyes and hair length that passed their shoulders with a centre parting. Claire and Michelle both had blonde hair; Danielle was a brunette. Danielle and Michelle stood around the same height of five feet five inches; Claire was shorter by four inches.

Drew had to admit, if only to himself, he quite liked Danielle. *Too young*, he would repeat in his mind. At thirty-one, that made him twelve years older. *Not too old... yes. Too old. Too old. Not made easy by the way she keeps looking at me. Bending over in front of me to pick up something that she, by* accident, *had dropped on the floor. Her behaviour has been equally as bad as her friends. How she looks in her blue bikini... too old. Too old. Even earlier today, she had again, by* accident, *dropped something on the floor. With her recent behaviour, although I've never done so before, could have yanked down her bikini panties and smacked her bottom hard. Walking in the bathroom whilst I'm drying myself after a shower... of course, by* accident. *If she ever does that again, I am taking her across my knee. Certainly over due. They've all pushed me too far. One more chance...*

Michelle had known Drew since her middle teens. She was a troubled youth who found it difficult to focus on her studies. As a teacher at her school, Drew decided he would tutor her and help her with her attitude brought on due to frustration at not being able to get to grips with some of her classes. Shortly after a year of knowing him, Drew and his wife, Jacqueline, were going through a divorce.

Two main areas that meant a lot to Drew were keeping fit and eating healthy; the other was teaching and helping troubled youths. Jacqueline grew jealous and increasingly angry with him when he spent time with the opposite sex.

Although he loved her dearly, he knew their relationship had to end. Additionally, he promised himself that he would not allow this event to distract him from what he enjoyed doing and what he did best.

Jacqueline never truly understood her husband's urging to help others. She could appreciate, if only a little, the value of being charitable; however, *there must be more to it than what he says*, she assumed. It was not as if Drew neglected her, but she wanted more.

There must be more than just helping *these unfortunates. An affair, perhaps?* she thought. In reality, this was nonsense.

They had been together for three years. In the heat of passion and the moment, only after six moths, they were married.

Their relationship, including marriage, began well. Unfortunately, Drew found himself putting so much energy into making the marriage work he gradually realised that no matter how much he gave, it was never enough; Jacqueline always wanted more while giving very little in return.

In his early twenties, and something that changed his life for the better, he served in Vietnam.

Drew was never one to talk about some of his unpleasant experiences, wanting to save his wife from experiencing them, if only in her mind. On the other hand, he did want to share an experience that resulted in his honourable discharge and receiving amongst his service medals, the Naval Cross along with the Purple Heart, both proudly received. Whenever he mentioned in this in conversation, Jacqueline always changed the subject rather bluntly. Drew appreciated that she was against the war, and fair enough, but to snap at him stating her lack of interest had always saddened him; a particular experience explained how he became the man he is today.

Her lack of interest in anything other than herself resulted in the inevitable. He wanted nothing more to do with her. This pleased her, and as far as Drew felt... *Good riddance... long overdue. One day, I'll find the right girl for me. For now, I will focus on helping others.*

On the receiving end of such help, Michelle agreed on extra homework and consequences for not doing so. Mowing the lawn or chores around his home was typical. He would sometimes ground her from social events, if he felt it was necessary. Reluctantly, she accepted these punishments. He did not have to help her, and after all, results of his tutoring were clear as she excelled in school. Michelle was grateful for such help and admired him immensely.

One time, Michelle misbehaved very badly, more so than ever before. She had only just turned eighteen. Drew knew she occasionally smoked pot and did not mind this. If he found anything stronger on her person, she would be in big trouble. This, he made very clear when he found a much more potent substance that had fallen out of her bag. He was furious and gave her a good scolding. He warned her of the dangers and made her promise never to do anything like that again. She was sorry for experimenting with such, swearing never to do so again.

He wanted to make himself even clearer. "You do anything like that again, my girl. Actually, you are now at an age where I should not even need to discipline you. Therefore, if you misbehave again, and trust me it'll be far worse if I ever catch you doing anything so dangerous..." He took a deep breath, uncertain if he would actually go through with it. He felt as if he could when he found such a dangerous substance. "I will take down your pants, put you across my knee and give you such a spanking."

No sooner had he finished, Michelle gasped, "You wouldn't?!"

"Yes, my girl, I would. I care about you too much to allow you to go off the rails. Now do I make myself clear?"

"Yes, sir, I will." Michelle blushed, not knowing where to look.

"Come here." He pulled her close and they hugged.

Michelle could tell he was serious. Not wanting to end up over his knee, she would make an effort not to put herself in a situation that may warrant it. She respected him for making such a firm decision with her.

Warning them several times, Drew decided to warn them for the last time and in a more firm manner not usually seen, "If you three do not pack it in, I promise you there will be spanked bottoms all round."

"Oooh… yes, please do," Danielle cheekily moaned, twisting on her side tapping her own bottom whilst she lay on her sun chair.

Claire and Michele were both unable to take Drew seriously; they began laughing.

"Oh, I see. Very well!" Not tolerating any more, he walked up to Michelle, took a firm grip on her arm and pulled her to her feet.

"What are you doing?" She said confused.

"You know damn well what I am doing, my girl. I told you what would happen and have warned you several times, nicely along with it!" His intention was to say no more until he had taken her across his knee. Michelle, suddenly realising her fate, had *a lot* to say but would not have enough time to do so.

Feelings of sheer terror rushed through her body at the thought of being spanked in front of her friends. So terrified, words that she wanted to say came out very differently. "Please no! No! N-wait! Sir, I'm Sorry! Not here, not now. Sir, please! Sir, no! S..."

With that final plea, Drew had arrived at the bench and table near by; he sat. Interrupting her, he scolded, "You better get across my knee, right now, young lady!"

Her terror grew, and as such, she froze to the spot. When again she spoke, her words were almost like a whisper. "Nooo! Please, sir."

Having had enough of her disobedience for one day, Drew leaned forward and removed his slipper-like shoes, one of which he decided to take hold of and place beside him for the time being.

Michelle's face turned red with embarrassment. Her next couple of words nearly overlapped one other as events happened so fast.

"No! Nooo!-Noooooo!"

The first *No* at this point was referring to when Michelle's mentor removed both his slippers and had taken hold of one of them; the second was when he gripped the sides of her bikini panties and pulled them down. This left a mortified Michelle exposed and naked below the waist, except for her bikini panties around her lower thighs; the third was when Drew hauled her across his knee.

From the angle of her friends, it had left them both very shocked, but also very curious. This was something they never expected to witness. Both kept throwing quick glances at each other before turning back to watch the spanking unfold.

Shocking as it was, it was also very exciting. As much as they both wanted to feel sorry for Michelle, they were more fascinated and thrilled as they watched their best friend dragged away, having her panties taken down, and then effortlessly taken across her mentor's knee. As an added bonus, it was very funny to see their best friend decrease in age, from a very confident young lady to a very scared little girl; the pleading language she used and her more or less co-operation, not even putting up a fraction of a fight.

From Michelle's point of view, it felt as if what just occurred was not real. It seemed like a dream and soon she would wake up. She could barely believe that this was actually going to happen to her. There was no escaping it. It was going to happen to her. A huge wave of embarrassment surged through her body making her cheeks flush even more... *If that was ever possible*, she thought. She knew her bottom would shortly match such a colour, and knowing this, her embarrassment amplified. If the spanking had occurred in private, it would still be embarrassing, but not so humiliating.

Then the situation became dire as she could not obey her mentor and lay across his knee. When Michelle saw him pick up one of his slippers, this was unthinkable.

Surely, his hand would be enough, wouldn't it?

Before Michelle had a chance to plead with any coherence, Drew had yanked down her bikini panties. In a split second, her whole world as she imagined had almost crumbled all around. It seemed as if a strong wind had come by and taken away her dignity. She felt a sudden breeze blow across her exposed bottom as her panties sharply came down. She wanted to say something, to say more than a predictable protest. Nothing came out apart from the repeated *No* in different forms.

Michelle tried to cover her front but had no time. Drew grabbed hold of her hand before she had a chance. One final protest was all she could muster before finding herself across his knee. Michelle felt her body move even though she could not. No longer frozen, Drew had easily put her into the appropriate position.

Laying bare bottom, across her mentor's knee, Michelle truly felt like the naughty girl she had behaved. Inside she felt she deserved it, thus was her reason for not struggling. He had been extremely patient with her and her friends. Although they did not know it, Michelle knew they were next. That gave her a little comfort.

Words of nearly two years ago rang in her ears. Words she had forgotten until now... 'I will take down your pants and put you over my knee.'

Michelle laid waiting as Drew picked up the slipper he placed beside him and under her left leg.

I will be a good girl and I will take this spanking like one. If I had behaved like I had promised, this would not be happening.

Tears already filled her eyes before the spanking had begun. She was determined not to put up a struggle and lay across her mentor's knee as obedient as she could. She would try not to cry. Chances were she knew she would. The spanking would hurt, but the tears would not be solely from the pain. More that she had pushed him this far in the first place.

Drew picked up one of his slippers and placed it against Michelle's bottom. He had never spanked before, but he knew it was the right thing to do.

Was it? Yes, he decided.

He would not allow her bad behaviour to continue and certainly not allow it to get any worse.

Raising his right arm, the slipper sharply whacked across her bottom making a loud whooping sound.

"OW! Ow! Ow! Ow!" Michelle yelped as the slipper whapped several times across her bottom.

Michelle had wanted to remain as quiet as she possibly could. This proved too difficult as wallop after wallop, Drew's slipper whacked down upon her bared bottom. The slipper connecting with her skin produced an almost burning feeling, which only got worse as the heat began to spread. It also had an added sting, which lingered on and increased with each new whack. Michelle's feelings grew of wanting so much to put her arm back to cover her bottom.

No, no, I will not, she determined.

Instead, she gripped firmly the bench and tried to think of something else. She tried and failed. All she could think about at this time was being across her mentor's knee and the pain across her bare bottom.

There was no choice in the matter of yelping and tears, which had already filled her eyes, began slowly falling down her face. Michelle tried her hardest not to wail, but she allowed herself to sob freely, hoping that soon the spanking would be over, even though it had not long begun.

"It is too awkward to use this thing," Drew remarked, referring to his slipper. He placed it behind him. "My hand will be more than enough, little one. It will soon be over. It may mean a slightly longer spanking since I'm using my hand, but we will see." With those words, the spanking continued.

Michelle was grateful that her mentor decided to go back to using his hand, still hard enough to be painful and leave a sting, but not as awful as that slipper. Then again, with a longer spanking, perhaps the slipper may have been best after all.

"Ah! Eee! Ah! Oww! Ow! Ow! Ow! Ow! Ahh!" Michelle inhaled deeply as Drew's hand sharply smacked across her bottom.

At this stage, Claire and Danielle were fixated on what

was taking place. Knowing how laid back Drew was, it was a total surprise. As much a shock it remained, they were still unable to look elsewhere. For both, a kind of morbid fascination about seeing their best friend in such a position and plainly accepting it, sobbing away (*pathetically*, Claire additionally thought) was too much for them to think of anything else.

The only kind of resistance from Michelle was when she bent her legs, though this seemed more a natural reaction rather than that of protesting, for when Drew scolded firmly, *Down!* or *Put your leg down, right now!* his words were met with instant obedience.

Drew noticed parts of her bottom become a deeper red with each smack and that almost her entire bottom was a bright red colour. He decided the spanking would not last much longer.

Still sobbing away, Michelle could only hope that it would end at any moment. It did not. When a moment was free in her mind to think, she knew of one thing, simply there *were* going to be changes in her behaviour... suddenly, another pause.

"I hope there will be some changes in your behaviour, my girl?"

Sniffing, she sobbed, "Y-yes... sir. I promise... I will... behave better. Please, no more," she managed to continue, breathless and trying to hold in as many tears as she could.

Drew pulled up her swimming panties and let her up and off his knee. Rubbing her own bottom, easing the sting only a little, Michelle again apologised. "I am... sorry, sir."

"I know, little one. Come here." Drew stood, pulled Michelle towards him, and gave her a big hug. "I am sorry, too. I just hope never to do this again."

Beginning to let out those tears, she buried her head into his chest and held onto him. "I will be a good girl, I promise," she muttered into his chest. Although Michelle's bottom was a bright red and stinging, she still preferred to hug than rub her bottom.

Rubbing her back, Drew spoke softly. "Come on, it's time you went to your room. If you want another hug, you may come and see me later."

"Yes, sir." Michelle once again rubbed her bottom and ran upstairs to her room as more tears began to appear. Reaching over to find a pot of cream, she looked in the mirror and viewed her well-spanked bottom. She slowly peeled down her panties, almost unable to take her eyes off what she saw in the reflection. She generously rubbed as much cream as she could into her burning cheeks.

Wanting only to throw herself onto her bed, rub her bottom some more whilst crying into her pillow, and then fall asleep, she knew very well that Danielle and Claire were next.

Moving towards the open window and peaking out, trying to remain very quiet and unseen, Michelle continued rubbing her bottom as she peered out the window to view her mentor move towards Claire.

"Stand up." Drew reached for Clare's arm and pulled her to her feet.

Her amusement of watching her friend's spanking turned to frustration. "Wait! What do you think you're doing?"

"You're next."

In those words, Danielle knew that she would follow; excitement grew inside her. She could run off whilst Claire received her spanking, but there was a desire felt that she had not even told either Michelle or Claire about. She wanted her bottom spanked. With a broad smile and leaning forward, she watched a much different reaction from Claire.

With an attempt to break away from Drew's firm grip on

her arm, she tried plucking away his fingers. Unlike Michelle, Claire determined not to have him take her easily across his knee. "Get off me!"

"Your behaviour has been just as bad, and it's about time you had your backside spanked."

Claire was relentless in trying to break away. She was hitting Drew's arm and tugging away, yelling at him, "Who the hell do you think you are? You are not spanking me. I'm not some wimp that will just lay there and take it! Get your hands off me, right now!"

Drew was surprised at the strength and will that Claire possessed. She certainly did not want a spanking.

It doesn't matter, she's getting one.

Straight after her last word of protest, Claire managed to tug herself loose. Although stunned, a little giggle came from both vantage points of Michelle and Danielle when they saw their friend fall backwards into the swimming pool.

After making a splash into the pool, Claire quickly surfaced. Most unhappy with her hair being soaked, she slapped the water, yelling, "Look what you've done! You ain't getting me now." Although not happy with the state of her hair, the water, however, did have its advantages. "I can't see you jumping in to get me. Ha!"

"You haven't outdone me yet, my girl. You cannot stay in there forever. And when you come out, you will be so sorry, I guarantee that." Drew was extremely angry with this little brat. She was short, but had spirit, which normally he would admire, save for such a moment as this. Claire was in need of a spanking and he was not going to let her of the hook so easy. "You have one minute to get out, Claire. If you do not, I will drain the pool." He stood, arms folded, waiting to see her next move.

A little more confident than she aught to have been,

Claire waded too close to the side of the pool. "I bet you can't even swim. Look at you," she said, sneeringly, "too frightened to jump in. Ha!" She shook her head, "What a joke!"

With a fast reflex, Drew bent down, flicked water into Claire's eyes, forcing them to close. "I'm sorry for that, sweetie." He said, not wanting to resort to this particular action, but it gave him the chance he needed. He grabbed a firmer hold of her arm this time and pulled her to the corner side of the pool; lifting her, he bent her over the edge.

The suddenness of having herself lifted out and bent over the edge of the pool surprised Claire. Her thoughts quickly focussed on her bottom, she stopped short of rubbing her stinging eyes when she felt a sudden breeze in that region. Whilst being lifted out, her swimming panties had fallen down. There was no chance in pulling them back up since they were floating on the water around her legs, which were still in the pool.

He moved much faster than Claire could have imagined that her mind scrambled. She was unsure of what to do next. With only her right hand available, she attempted to cover her bottom. She could not get up since Drew had his hand on her back.

Drew knew exactly what he wanted to do. Whilst Claire was smart mouthing him in the pool, he quickly decided on a course of action.

Still crouching, he moved Claire's hand away from her bottom with his left hand, and with his right, he gave her half a dozen hard whacks to her newly exposed beautiful area. The impact made a much louder smacking noise due to her wet bottom. The wetness made the slaps more painful, and in addition, the sting lingered on a little longer than it would otherwise.

Claire could only yelp; she was stuck. An attempt to

kick her legs and make a splash to slow down the spanking was a non-starter since she could not get her legs out of the pool in a way she would want.

Only wearing shorts and a t-shirt, getting a little wet was not much of a worry for Drew. He proceeded to sit on the corner edge of the pool. Whilst lifting and moving Claire, he put her across his left knee; the other leg he let dangle into the pool to trap her legs.

Drew did not hesitate to continue the spanking. One after the other and alternating between cheeks, he kept up a fast and solid pace.

With a good view on the other side of the pool sat Danielle. Needing to catch her breath when she saw how fast Drew moved, she loved every second. So much more than Michelle's spanking. She had a perfect view of Claire's trapped bare bottom, her legs mostly in the water. It was amusing, but not near as much as it was a turn on at being able to witness her friend's rounded bottom trying to avoid Drew's hand, wiggling from left to right. The loud smacking sound and the yelping of Claire's helplessness, still defiant and putting up a struggle, to no avail, made herself tingle with excitement.

From the window, Michelle was enjoy the drama unfold, still rubbing her sore bottom. She could clearly see the panic in Claire's face. Her friend attempted to cover her bottom again, but in doing so, made it easier for Drew to pin down both hands behind her back. There was nowhere to go. Michelle could see Claire trying to free her hands, but could only concentrate on the sting across her bottom as Drew speedily and heavily continued spanking.

Michelle grinned at the look on Claire's face, recalling very well the smile and the additional shake of the head, wondering why she had not put up a struggle.

Claire's mouth was open and would often close her eyes

and grit her teeth as the pain began to increase. Her eyes would open wide in combination with taking a deep breath.

One thing Claire did not want to do was beg him to stop. She would struggle as much as she could. This was damn near impossible in itself, let alone any chance of escape, trapped as she was. She attempted to wriggle her bottom to avoid the heavy smacking.

"You've been behaving just as bad as Michelle," Drew scolded as his hand continually rained down upon her bottom. "You wiggling your bottom will not make a slight bit of difference. You deserve every one of these, my girl."

When Claire's bottom seemed to dry up, Drew decided he would change that. He scooped a handful of water, poured it onto her right bottom cheek, and rubbed it in for a moment. He repeated a couple of times, and then did the same for her left cheek. She did have a nice smooth bottom, he noticed, but was too cross with her to appreciate it.

Grateful of a break in the spanking, Claire thought it was over and gave a sigh of relief. She would soon be greatly disappointed when Drew commenced. "What makes you even think it's over yet, my girl?"

"Oh, please, G-No!" Claire cried out. The brief relief she felt soon disappeared and tears came to her eyes.

Frantically trying to escape, she began to wriggle even harder. Once again, it was to no avail. Drew noticed how cute it looked to see her bottom become the only thing she could move. Viewing its desperate plight as it transformed to a brighter shade of red, Claire began breathing heavily. As he had expected, she was running out of energy.

Claire, with watery eyes, burst into tears. "Please," she said, sniffing. "Please, no. I'm sorry, sir."

Drew continued spanking for about a minute more. He let go of her hands and allowed her to lay her head into her arms. She continued crying and lay limp, thinking it cannot last much longer.

"I hope there will be serious changes, not only in your attitude, but also behaviour." Drew spoke more softly as he slowed down the spanking pace.

Claire raised her head for a moment and took another deep breath. "Yes... there will be. I'll try, I'll try. I will." Lowering her head into her arms, she let the tears flow as they came.

Drew stopped spanking. "I believe you. Good girl." He moved his right leg and lifted Claire so that she was lying across his full lap, and allowed her to cry for a few minutes. Drew allowed himself a short break to massage and rest his right arm. After a few minutes, when Claire's crying had turned to a whimper, he gently tapped her bottom. "You may get up now."

As she stood, Claire realised her panties were in the pool and covered her private area with one hand. With the other, just as frantically as she wriggled her bottom to avoid Drew's hand, she rubbed it with the same vigour, only pausing briefly when she walked up to Drew giving him a big hug. "Thank you, sir."

Not expecting Claire to be grateful for the spanking, judging from her behaviour beforehand, he nearly forgot to return the hug. She clearly had learned her lesson.

She sniffed. "I promise, sir, I'll be more respectful."

Whilst crying across his lap, she had time to think and reflect on her behaviour. Claire had a newly founded respect for Drew. She did not want him to think anything but good of her. She was very sorry, though her bottom felt even more so.

Drew spoke softly. "Come on, in you go," he said as he kissed her forehead. "Dry yourself. You'll catch pneumonia if you don't."

"Yes, sir." Claire happily obeyed, walking fast into the

house and upstairs, rubbing her bottom along the way.

She found a towel in the bathroom and wrapped it around her. The warmth of the towel felt good, the only exception was around her bottom. She wrapped a smaller towel around her head to dry her hair.

Heading into the bedroom, Claire walked over to her friend and gave her a hug. "Sorry for the look I gave you earlier."

"It's okay," Michelle said. "I just hope both our bottoms feel better soon. Can't talk to guys with a spanked bottom. That wouldn't impress them, I'd imagine, if they see it," she thought aloud.

"I dunno about that. After all, they may even like it. Perhaps even find it cute," Claire said with optimism, nervously laughing.

"Yes, let's hope." Michelle said, agreeing with her friend in the same manner. "The cream's on the bed. Help yourself."

As soon as she saw it, Claire picked it up, lifted her towel and applied a copious amount to her stinging bottom.

Michelle pressed her forefinger to her lips and pointed to the window. "Shh... come here."

Realising that Michelle must have seen her spanking, Claire blushed, even though she knew Danielle had, and it was likely that Michelle would have been watching from the window anyway.

Drew sat on the bench and rested for a few minutes. His shorts were wet along with half his t-shirt. Although a strong man, he still needed to allow his arm to rest.

He glanced towards Danielle, who was still sitting on her sun bed. A thought was running through his mind as he looked at her. She was leaning forward, a little out of breath, and with her head slightly lowered, was keeping eye contact with him. This was not what he had expected. She could have run off, but had not. She still could. He had noticed when he looked up for a moment whilst spanking Claire, that Danielle was breathing faster and not taking her eyes away. She had what seemed, on reflection of events, a certain level of enjoyment in her eyes.

More than enjoyment. Excitement. That's the word I was looking for.

That excitement had doubled. The look on her face had made this very clear.

Initially, there was no excitement for Drew when he spanked Michelle. It was implementing some much-needed discipline. For Claire, although the same, it was more challenging and certainly more satisfying smacking her bare bottom, and in particular, adding a greater sting as the water made it wet and then damp. Nevertheless, it was still discipline. On reflection, he experienced a small level of enjoyment; this had surprised him. The thought of spanking Danielle, however, was different; there was a level of eagerness. It was strange because he had never thought of spankings as something that would be a turn on, yet he was looking forward to this, which made him feel guilty. For a moment, he contemplated not doing so at all, but quickly realised since he had spanked two of the girls, he could not allow her to get away with her recent behaviour.

Drew sighed. Looking up at the sky, he had noticed two heads at an open window. "Get your heads back inside, young ladies," he said as he stood. "You will close the window, close the curtains, and lay on your beds. If I see you looking out one more time, I will head up there and spank the pair of you again, do I make myself clear?"

"What... no fair!" Michelle called out. "She saw us, so we should get to see her..."

Drew had no intention in spanking either of them, at that point or ever again, but he still took a step towards the house. In that moment, the window closed sharply, followed by the curtains. What Drew did not see, as he turned towards Danielle, was a pair of brats peeking through the lower half of the curtain.

Michelle did have a point, Drew thought, but he could not allow the two girls to view their friend enjoying it. Nor for that matter any enjoyment from him.

Danielle had begun to feel impatient. She wanted her bottom spanked, and spanked now. Would she need to throw herself across his lap? Exhaling deeply, the words she was dying to hear came.

"Come here, Danielle." No matter how much he would enjoy this, Drew was going to make sure it was a punishment. It would certainly feel like one.

At a fast pace, Danielle stood and walked over with a smile as she willingly took hold of his outstretched hand.

Drew led her inside his house and into the living room, and sat down on his footrest. He patted his lap. "Come on, little one, over you go."

"Yes, sir." Danielle spoke softly. She was yearning to replace *sir* with *Daddy*, but would not. She did not want Drew to be her actual dad, of course not. What she wanted was a man, not some of the puny boys she knew; a man who was kind and gentle, yet strong and knew when to be firm with her; someone who could take care of her. She was attracted to him, very much so. She found it ironic that there was no place she could imagine more safe and secure than having Drew exposing her bare bottom whilst over his knee.

Wanting to make the most of a moment that had finally arrived, she slowly peeled down her panties and removed them completely. She placed her hands on his lap and gently lay herself over. "I know that I have been a naughty little girl. Please give me a spanking."

She was doing this on purpose, Drew sighed.

He could tell that she knew he was going to enjoy this. It would be hard for her not to feel it. He could not help but admire the view as she removed her panties, which he originally planned on taking down after Danielle was over his knee. He could also not help being attracted to her, but it would not affect the outcome. She revealed a neatly shaved and trimmed vertical stripe in her lower region. He had not looked at another woman with such feelings since his ex-wife. He remembered how she completely shaved her pubic area. He preferred that, but Danielle had something extra about her that... *Stop it! She is too young. Twelve years too young. Not so much younger. Same age gap as my own parents. Danielle did have an amazing little bottom. Worth spanking. Needing some discipline. Even if she'd enjoy it... I would... stop it!*

Drew shook his head, snapping himself back to the matter at hand. He was ashamed to have such thoughts. Danielle was clever enough to know this and was not willing to help ease how he felt. He knew she had a crush on him, which again made the spanking more awkward, especially since it was very clear it was what she wanted.

As firm as he could, he replied, "You will think a lot different, my girl, when I am finished with you."

"Yes, sir. Sorry, sir. As always, you are right. My little bottom must be severely dealt with." Danielle said, grinning, knowing how she would sound and that it would make him spank her even harder. Even though she wanted a spanking, she also knew she would not be smiling when... *When he gets into the swing of it, pun intended*, she thought.

Shaking his head again, Drew found Danielle so damn cute. He wanted to get this spanking over with as soon as possible, which would not be easy since she was due a long and hard one. Additionally, he wanted it to last. With a desire to caress her beautiful little bottom and a struggle to resist, it became clear he needed to begin, and do so quickly. "You will be sorry, little one. You can trust me on that."

Danielle knew this would be painful, but felt in heaven over his knee. It was not a difficult task to find boys her own age willing to indulge her interest, some highly enthusiastic. She would always wind up disappointed. It was not the same. There was something much better about it this time. Maybe she would find someone else who could satisfy that spanking need, but for now, she had found what she wanted with Drew. She had a feeling that he would deliver what she wanted. Subsequently, with hope, he would want more.

With a cuteness that was Danielle, she wriggled her little bottom, encouraging Drew to begin.

Exhaling deeply, he patted her bottom for aim, and began.

With each smack against her smooth bottom, Drew noticed downstairs, he was growing harder and harder. He could feel the smoothness of her small but fleshy bottom, which did not make it easy. The heat, as it gradually increased, he lost count of the amount of times his hand whacked across each cheek, not that he counted with the other girls. His eyes fixated on the wobbling effect of his hand firmly and constantly smacking across her bottom.

As it became a brighter red, Drew focussed on other areas of her bottom that had not been touched or barely been spanked.

Drew was enjoying this immensely. He almost forgot to scold Danielle for her naughtiness, even though his hand spoke volumes. "I hope, little one," he scolded, still spanking. "I am sending a clear message for you to behave yourself."

"Ah! Ow! Yes, sir, you are, you are. Ow! Ah! Ah! Yes!

Yes, don't stop."

Even though a very painful spanking, and one lasting longer than that of the two other girls, it surprised Drew that she had such a high pain threshold; perhaps it was because she was enjoying it. Nonetheless, she could feel tears in her eyes, which brought along an added bonus for her.

Managing to spank her harder, speaking more firmly, he scolded, "I have no intention of stopping, my girl. You have far from learned your lesson!" Drew was certainly enjoying himself, but would still make Danielle cry and plead to stop. After all, he was disciplining her. It was clear she was enjoying it, even though in pain. There was a near by mirror, and in its reflection, he could see her eyes closed and mouth open; her face was a mixture of pleasure and pain. Each yelp had a touch of delight to it, and he wanted to make sure this little brat got the spanking she deserved, and turn it around to become more painful than pleasurable.

Danielle began to feel Drew's hand more so at this stage, which made her yelp and yell out even louder. He began to spank the back of her thighs, which also began to make it more painful. No sooner had Drew began to think it would never happen, tears appeared and fell from her eyes.

"I am glad to see the desired effect, little one." He was satisfied that the spanking was showing some results. "This better be a lesson you will not forget in a hurry."

"Yes, sir." Sniffing through tears, Danielle sobbed, "I am learning."

I am *learning*, she thought; learning she wanted him to take her across his knee more often.

An effort to drive home, he noticed a hairbrush, that was next to the footrest. He halted the spanking for a moment as he picked it up. "I believe this, little one," Drew said, patting the brush against each cheek, "will drive home a much needed disciplinary session."

Gasping, and then taking a deep breath, Danielle braced herself. With what seemed so much more painful against her already very tender little bottom, the spanking started to feel as a punishment. Before she had expected, the effect of the hairbrush was making her scream. Just when it seemed more painful than pleasure, her body began to shake over Drew's lap. She could feel how wet she was as she came to orgasm.

Drew had not seen such a thing happen, and it turned him on considerably. He wanted to discipline this little brat, and had succeeded in such a task, but had also brought her to orgasm. An urging desire to caress her bottom along with a greater urge to do much more had grown as hard as his manhood, which Danielle could feel against her.

She opened and closed her legs to heighten the sensation, and raised her legs so her body could feel more of Drew's hardness against her.

Drew, in order to help withstand the need to feel her down below, as he could see how swollen and moist she had become, landed the hairbrush upon her bottom several more times.

As her orgasms multiplied, she screamed out with a combination of immense pain and pleasure, her bottom feeling numb with a warm sensation flowing through her body. She wanted to feel Drew inside her, though she dared not ask.

As Danielle's orgasms faded, she remained breathless over his knee, sobbing. "I will try to behave in future, sir."

He was out of breath himself. "Good girl. I forgive you for your naughtiness and hope this won't be necessary any time soon, if at all." He lifted Danielle off his lap, sat her on it, and gave her a big hug. She cried into his chest for a couple of minutes, feeling how uncomfortable it was to sit, but was happy to sit on Drew's lap.

"I will forget about your behaviour whilst over my knee as well, young lady. Now go up stairs. Put some clothes on. Then tell Michelle and Claire to do the same if they have not already done so, and come down here."

"Thank you, sir." After picking up her panties, Danielle walked upstairs, enjoying rubbing her bottom, albeit not the thought of sitting any time soon.

Drew could see her entire bottom and upper thighs that he had spanked a deep scarlet. He knew full well Danielle would do something naughty to earn another spanking. Part of him looked forward to it. However, he could not be certain if he could hold back from doing more than that and give her what she wanted. He exhaled at the thought. In addition, after enjoying the third spanking, he knew he could never use that as form of punishment again. There was too much risk in enjoying it. It would be different with Danielle, of course.

He slipped on his jeans, which were hanging over the chair, and finally caught back his breath. It had been a little tiring, more so than he expected, spanking all three in a row.

Danielle informed Michelle and Claire of what Drew had told her. She quickly put on her jeans before either one could see how much she was spanked.

"What took you so long? We couldn't hear anything from up here," Michelle asked, concerned.

"Your mentor needed a break before he spanked me. But," she said, wanting to change the subject, "I think we should all do as he says and get downstairs quickly."

"Don't you want to put some cream on?" Claire asked.

"It's okay. I'll do that a little later." In truth, Danielle enjoyed the stinging and burning sensation in her bottom.

They all put some clothes on, went downstairs, and stood next to each other.

"Right, young ladies. I have never spanked before and do apologise for doing so now. I don't feel particularly good about it," he said... *Except for Danielle*, he thought. "I can't expect you to think highly of me. I accept that. If you wish, there is no need to discuss this further or even remember that it happened at all. But that is your decision to make and not mine. I'll give you all some money so you can go out, either later or now, and make the most of what started as a good day."

Including Danielle, Drew was beginning to regret the spankings. *Even though they deserved it... perhaps.*

None of them had expected such a speech from him. They all, in fact, respected him a little more for it, both the speech and the spanking. They all went over and gave him a big hug, apologising once more.

Not wanting it to come across as a cheesy moment, Michelle decided to delay what she wanted to say for when the other two left the house before joining them to enjoy the remainder of the day. She walked towards her mentor and gave him another big hug, wanting to remind him she did not hate him for spanking her, knowing he regretted it.

Claire was surprised that she felt admiration for Drew after he had taken her in hand. She realised they all had overstepped the line, consequently deserving a sore bottom in return.

As for Danielle, she was very sorry for her behaviour; however, she had not learned her lesson for long. As the burning sting from her bottom faded, she desperately yearned to have that feeling once again. When her bottom had time to heal, she was determined to find time to be alone with Drew and make him spank her again. More than anything, she wanted to proceed further than just a spanking. Maybe it would happen, but he did have a lot of self-control. Besides, she wanted the approval of Michelle before attempting such a thing. At some point in the near future, she would mention that she had a minor crush, albeit much more, on her friend's mentor, and judge her reaction.

I will find a way to be with him… as for telling Michelle, well, I can always take it back as a joke… not that I need her approval in all this. He will be mine. Time will tell.

Mediaeval Desires
(A Wars of the Roses spanking story)
~Brat No. 4: Christiana~

The weather was unbelievable. There had been a blizzard, and the snow that covered all around made it more difficult to navigate. The wounds inflicted upon Carver added to his pain. Cold, hunger and exhaustion made it even more difficult to find the strength to move. He knew he must. Dying was not an option. He must continue… *But where?* He did not know this countryside. As far as he was concerned, anywhere could lurk a person willing to slit his throat, be it either a thief with eyes on an easy purse or the enemy; perhaps even a soldier that would have once fought alongside him might want to rob so easy a target.

This was a part of the Lancastrian heartland, was it not? Was it? His confusion increased.

I could easily have wandered in the wrong direction and towards the Yorkist camp. Unlikely? He was not sure and unable to think straight.

Being so dark, it must be gone midnight.

Any normal day he would know what to do. He had though, survived a day that was by far no ordinary day, that Palm Sunday, 29 March 1461.

Carver thought it best to drop anything that could identify for whom he fought. Best to play circumstance as it occurred. He kept his dagger, a sword he took from a near dead soldier after losing his in the route, his longbow and a few arrows that remained in his quiver. It was more than likely he would need to hunt to stay alive. In his present state that seemed near impossible.

There was a village near by.

Perhaps with fortune, I may pay someone for a place to stay. In every town or village, one could always find an inn. Whether they had any room, and depending if they were friendly or believed I was on the side for which I would need to claim, would be a matter of life or death, he thought wearily.

He was feeling weaker by the minute, which deepened his confusion, but not to a point where he became unaware that if he stayed in the open for much longer such a decision would swiftly be made for him.

The freezing weather prevented his wounds from infection, as they would have if it had been a blistering hot summer day. He was grateful for that. *I am still alive... for now.*

Falling to his knees, he crawled through the snow; a trail of blood followed him. The pain that spread in many directions throughout his entire body had found itself replaced with that of numbness. The wound to his face, from the side of his left eye straight down to his jaw, was near fatal. Another wound across his left arm and right leg impeded his crawl.

Tiredness over came him, but he knew he must stay

awake, for if he fell asleep it was unlikely that he would wake in this world. He wanted to find a tree in a forest to rest against; however, the Yorkist soldiers still were hunting the remaining Lancastrians.

Perhaps they were not. It was not worth finding out.

"Keep moving. Keep moving," he told himself, clutching a lock of hair he had taken from the last person he killed whilst fleeing during the route. It was a lock of hair from a fair-headed girl. Young, he assumed. It showed no sign of greying. It would no doubt be the last time he would caress a girl's hair.

Carver had no idea where he was heading or even where he was. He would grab handfuls of snow and put them in his mouth. The freezing snow melting in his mouth was very much welcome. However, it made him feel even colder, and that was not welcome, but necessary all the same. He felt extremely dehydrated and confused.

Was it better to eat more snow, feel more awake, and gain more energy? Perhaps I should not. In its place, maybe I should keep as warm as I am able, and thus stay alive a little longer. Yet if I did that, I would move much slower, and that would not get me to where I wanted in time, wherever that was... would it? He was not sure of much anymore.

Carver's eyes slowly began to close. His movement became even slower until he could move no longer. Turning on his back, he looked to the white covered sky. He spoke a prayer, but found it difficult to speak. Clutching the lock of hair, he prayed for forgiveness for the blood he had spilled. He continued, praying for the souls of those killed. He was repentant, and hoped God would not judge him too harsh. He had always wanted a peaceful life, but as he knew, *Life was not always what one wanted, more what one made from what was granted him*, his father would say. Some day he would like to pursue his desires. It depended on whether or not he survived the day out. Surviving so far was a good sign. All he needed to do was to survive a little longer.

His last thoughts were of wanting to find a girl with whom to share a true connection. Carver was fortunate with good looks to match his brave nature. His two-and-twenty-year-old broad and tall frame added to his warrior presence. Searching for a girl who found these qualities attractive was easy. There was much more to him than that. He had fought in battles and had killed many. Even so, it was his desire for a peaceful life that made him seek a girl who understood him, and as important, wanted to join him in such a life. In a jovial manner, Carver would mention his plans, and from whatever the reaction of the girl, it would tell him if that girl was the right one for him. He had come close, but no such fortune for exactly what he yearned for; hard to describe, but he would know if ever there was such a girl. For the moment, he enjoyed the company of many whilst yearning for the one whom would truly understand him.

Realising that perhaps it was not meant to be, he prepared to pass on into the next world. He closed his eyes and died... or so he thought.

Gradually opening his eyes, Carver saw a bright light, but it was a candle light, and beyond that, there was a huge fireplace. Confused, he attempted to raise himself and sit upright. This was not as easy as he had expected; the pain coursing through muscles made it impossible.

"Shh... do not attempt to move." Carver felt a smooth hand caress his forehead and hair accompanying the soft female voice. "I've been waiting to look upon your eyes. I'm pleased to discover they are blue, my favourite colour. And the same as mine. I talk too much."

"No. Do continue. I am not going anywhere." Glad to

be alive and finally warm, he allowed this kind girl to rest the sheets over his arms. He relaxed himself and delighted in closing his eyes. Still not easy to talk, he managed, "Whilst I gather strength, do tell me about yourself and how you..." He suddenly began coughing. The kind girl lifted his head and gave him some water. Feeling relieved, he relaxed once more.

"How I came to find you?" she said, finishing his sentence for him.

"Aye. You are very clever." Carver gave a slow deliberate wink that made the kind girl blush and lower her head. "But first, your name. I am Carver. In addition, I am of two-and-twenty-years. You appear very youthful, but would rather not guess at your age. You know mine, let me know yours."

"My name is Christiana."

"Ah... that is a beautiful name. Argh, my head!" Carver held both hands to the sides of his head. "What was in that drink, Geneva liquor?" he said, managing to smile briefly before the pain increased.

"Here." With haste, Christiana helped Carver lean forward, giving him a herbal mixture that would ease the pain in his head. "Calm yourself," she ordered, sweetly. "Your wounds are healing. However, the pain will arrive and disappear for the present. You have accomplished much in surviving thus far. I will tell you about myself only if you promise to calm yourself and not attempt anything in haste."

She had a way in which her words, softly spoken and with such compassion, and considering he could do nothing at such a time, Carver allowed her to help him lay down. He closed his eyes again. "I will do as you wish. Your sweet voice will no doubt assist in my healing."

Carver could not see Christiana's face as she blushed and

smiled once more. She ran her fingers through his dark hair and sat on a stool beside him. "I am of years nineteen. I am married, though for how long, be in God's hands. I was married to him when I was fifteen. Acel. He was wealthy and had taken a liking to me. My family was in financial difficulty, and as an obedient and loving daughter, loyal to my family, I did not resist. In truth, I had no choice, but pretended to be pleased." She paused and sighed.

Carver wanted to say something reassuring. Christiana made it plain the lack of joy she felt as she spoke of her husband. He kept his eyes closed, not wanting to see the pain in her eyes. He was too weak to act upon urges to offer assistance with her plight. "I am sorry to hear of your predicament." Carver felt for her hand and rested his against hers. "Do continue."

Taking a deep breath and exhaling deeply, Christiana continued. "I was young and attractive."

"Still are, sweet lady," Carver interrupted. He opened his eyes a little before closing them, and was pleased to catch a glimpse of her smile.

"Rest. Or I *will* provide you with Geneva liquor in place of a herbal remedy. I have no doubt you will enjoy the drink, but it will do your head no favours in your condition." It was Christiana's turn to be pleased to see him smile. "I am not able to speak with my husband in such a manner. I am glad I can with you.

"To continue. I was young and attractive, and being the pleasant girl that I am, Acel fast found himself attracted to me. Acel had recently bought an estate near where I lived. He was just over twice my age, and as an extremely wealthy man, he was more than eager to lighten our financial burden. It was clear he had feelings towards me. It was not long before he was seeking my hand in marriage. With knowledge that it was the wishes of my parents and would enable security for my father, mother and sister, as I mentioned earlier, I had no choice. I was soon betrothed. There was one thing I did have a choice regarding. I chose to remain dignified throughout, and as far as anyone knew, I was in good spirits and eager to marry.

"In truth, I knew not what I wanted. Acel appeared as a genuinely kind man with good intentions. I had a deep feeling that something was not well with our match. I thought that perhaps I was wrong. Perhaps, after all, I would be happy. He was an attractive man, but there was something not right. I learned when we were discussing his mistress, at least one of them, and him spending too much time with her on his return from France. He would not tell me her name, saying it was not my place to ask. When I perused the issue, he was more than happy to allow me to discover my place. As you may imagine, I am not able to neither begin nor finish a brawl. He is not only good at fighting men, but women, too." Christiana saw Carver's eyes open suddenly.

"Is he, indeed?" He had no intention in hiding his displeasure. Carver was with haste was harbouring feelings for this kind and softly spoken girl that saved his life. The thought of losing such a girl to such a man was more pain than he already felt. To make it worse it was only due to his wealth that this *Ass* found it possible to have this wonderful girl. Even with the blessed fortune of having her in his life, he mistreats her. That was not acceptable. Carver could appreciate her family predicament, but still, money spoke more than love. Carver was not naïve. He knew the way of the world. It did not ease his anger at hearing Acel's treatment of her. "Where, pray tell, is his location?"

"Shh... rest. All shall be revealed in due time. More than you presently realise."

"Where is he? I am in pain, but that be of little importance if you compare to how I shall deal with him." Carver began to rise, but his wounds rendered him unable.

Christiana raised her voice a little, still managing to sound sweet. She stood and stepped backwards. "Stop!" She held her hand to his chest. "You must do nothing. I had hoped you would be wiser than that. Do not have me feeling wrong about you as well."

Carver noticed the sadness that filled her face. Looking into her eyes, he felt remorse at his sharp actions.

This is, indeed, a very sweet girl. Fragrance, charm and looks.

He lay back, and with a deep breath, calmed himself. "I am usually much wiser than that. I did not mean to startle you. I shall say, my sweet girl, do not accuse me of being anything like him. I would not harm you in any way." This was no time for humour, he felt; however, *In a way, you are in need of a little.* "So, it would seem that this..." Carver said, pretending to forget her husband's name, "*Ass?*" He half pronounced it correctly.

"... el." Christiana finished off the pronunciation.

"*Ass!*" he insisted.

She nearly corrected him again, but, and with a nod, she silently agreed.

"Not only an ass, be an 'assle, too." He was pleased to see her smile, accompanied with an equally cute little giggle. "Though, having said that, I believe it is insulting to all donkeys, rather than the other way around."

Giggling again, she took hold of his hand.

Pleased to laugh in what seemed a long while and with his decision to rest, still holding his hand, Christiana sat. "I would hope you do not mean that. Harming me, I mean." To ease Carver's confused expression, she continued. "I mean... I want to let you know... I may as well be plain. I, without doubt, dislike Acel's behaviour towards me, physical or otherwise. I do not seek a man to beat me." Christiana felt highly nervous at expressing her desires, but wanted and needed to take such a chance. "However, I do like the thought of a man who is masterful, yet in a pleasant way. To find a man that can allow me to be myself, but not allow me to behave too much like a brat. For the present, I must be aware of every action I take, never to feel at ease, and I grow ever increasingly tired.

"I would like to experience a firm hand across my bottom when it is needed. Even to lay myself down upon his lap and have my naked bottom receive a good walloping. But with love. I do not know if it is possible to find such a man. To combine such whilst being treated like a princess and have the outside world know not or even suspect my desires." Christiana became embarrassed and looked down. "Silly, I know. I should go. I need to look upon my husband, and..."

Carver squeezed her hand. "No, my sweet girl. You will stay," he said, as firm as he could, still very much weak. Christiana's head remained lowered. "Your desires are not silly. There is no reason why you should not want such a dream for yourself. You have a husband, yes. Nevertheless, he is not worthy of you. This is most certain; he does not deserve either yourself or what love you may have for him. I would not act as he does and would not want to harm you in any way, yet if you desire a walloping to your bottom, but in a loving manner, I would be more than pleased to do so. If it pleases you, it pleases me. Besides, I like the sound of it."

Christiana raised her head slowly and smiled. "I need to check upon," she paused, letting out a sigh. "Acel. I will return soon and we shall speak more. You need more rest. It will be at such a time I shall continue."

As Christiana stood, Carver beckoned her to come

closer. Laying down he was still able to take her hand and pull her close to him. He kissed her hand. "I look forward to it. You truly are a gift from God. Mine to you. Allowing another man to kiss you whilst you are married, even though was only the hand, knowing your feelings for myself is very naughty, my girl, indeed." Smiling, he turned her around and gave her bottom a single smack.

"Ow!" Christiana yelped, sounding cute. She could not help her wide smile. "Yes, my lord." She left the room and made her way upstairs to check upon Acel.

My lord... Carver enjoyed the sound of her sweet soft voice referring to him as such. Very formal. *Apt*, he thought. *Considering her chosen desires.*

He attempted to sleep, though as Christiana flooded his thoughts, this in itself became a challenge. He gave a silent prayer to dream about her. Not long thereafter, coincidental, he knew, there was a pleasant answer to his prayer.

Throughout the next few weeks, Carver and Christiana talked for as long as time permitted. Interruptions came from sleep and the rest that Carver needed in order to gain strength. Christiana would also take care of her ailing husband. She hated referring to Acel as such, especially since she became increasingly close to Carver.

Nearly a fortnight later, after Christiana had prepared food for Carver while he slept, an urge that had built itself up inside of her was something she could no longer resist.

Her conversations with Carver had been brief in this time due to Acel's failing health and constantly in needed of her attention. This attention was not only a constant source of interruption, but frustration, too.

Sitting at his bedside, as she had done several times before, she enjoyed watching him sleep. She lightly nudged him to find out if he was in deep sleep. It appeared that he was. Quietly, or as quiet as the floorboards allowed, she stood and crept her way around the bed to his right side, and knelt on the bed. A combination extreme nervousness, excitement and curiosity were raging within as she made her decision to do what she had wanted to do the moment she began speaking with Carver.

She wore a plain green dress, which although a simple item of clothing, suited her for when she was taking care of Carver and Acel. She would not wear such in public, but around her home for the time being it would suffice. She remained as beautiful as ever. Her hands slowly raised her dress, exposing herself naked from below the waist. Gently, as to not wake Carver, she lay across his lap as he slept on his back.

It was as if heaven itself had lay presented before her. Christiana felt so comfortable across his large strong lap, and with her bare bottom raised as if ready for discipline, excited her so much more. Feelings of an erotic nature filled her. She was behaving in a manner that warranted discipline, which incidentally, was what she wanted. Her bottom hungered for Carver's hand.

Something felt right about this man. She was not a strong woman, but felt that she could not allow anyone to prevent her from taking away the heavenly feelings she felt at that precise moment.

Wanting to lay there for a lot longer, Christiana knew she must get up. As she began to raise herself, she felt a hand pushing her back down and another whacking her bottom. Four times, in fast succession came as such a surprise she tried to move, but could not; only gasp and cry out in disbelief that he caught her in such a compromising position. She felt so embarrassed at exposing herself. She wanted to bury her head with her hair. Instead, with a sharp turn, wide eyed and mouth opened, she looked towards Carver, whom clearly was awake.

"Without a doubt, my sweet one, you are a misbehaving girl. If I had the strength, your bottom would be in serious trouble." In truth, Carver was awake ever since she gently nudged him. He pretended to be asleep, closing his eyes enough to feign sleep, yet still manage to watch this beautiful girl position herself across his lap. It was a pleasure. He enjoyed watching this otherwise shy girl expose herself from below the waist. "When I," he said, not as firmly as he would have liked, "have recovered enough strength, you will lay once more across my lap. Pray tell me you understand, my sweet girl."

"Aye, my lord. I am so sorry. I just, I just wanted-Ow!"

"You will remain silent for the moment. Acknowledging that you understand is all that I seek, my sweet girl." Carver began to caress her beautifully shaped bottom. His hand drifted gently across and around her smooth exposed hide. Such treatment was most welcome by Christiana. She obediently said nothing. "In truth, I was awake. And I will admit it felt a heavenly experience as you laid yourself across my lap. I will, in time, need to learn how to separate discipline from the erotic. I suspect it will not be easy. And as much as this was enjoyable, I shall need to discipline you for doing so at a later time. You may raise yourself." Carver stopped caressing Christiana's bottom, not at all easy being so beautiful, and allowed her to move.

"Aye, sir. Thank you, Carver." As she moved from the bed and around the other side to sit on the stool, Christiana allowed her dress to fall down naturally. She still felt embarrassed, but was comfortable to feel so in Carver's presence. "I have prepared something for you. Whilst you eat, I will tell you more. First, what is your full name? You have always avoided the topic of conversation and whenever I mention it, you hastily change the subject. I want to hear it. I assume it is not Carver Carver, is it not?" She smiled, her cheeks still flushed.

"It is not. I just do not like it. Call me by my first name and I will wallop your hide, my girl. Humphrey."

"Humphrey. What is so wrong with that? Ah..." Her mouth opened wide, immediately realising her mistake.

"Stand up. Come on, stand up, sweet one."

Christiana obediently stood and turned. Carver sat himself up, pleased that without the need for him to tell her, she raised her dress and stuck out her bottom in his direction. She was eager to receive his loving hand. He walloped each bottom cheek, the sound combined with that of the crackling fire, was rather pleasant to both their ears. "You may now sit. And remember, sweet one, I do not like that name."

"I do," she protested. "And if you wish to have me, you will need to become accustomed to it," she dared to say.

"Tell me, my sweet one, which one of us needs to be obedient?"

"I have no illusions in answer to that, sir." Christiana genuinely liked the name. Whether present or future, most times she would want to obey Carver. Other times she would not. This would be one of those times. "But I still maintain..."

"Speak no more of this," Carver interrupted. "You are correct." He paused shortly. "I like how you can be challenging and yet at the same time know how to present your bottom when in need of a walloping. You are undeniably a very special girl. Pass me the food, if you will, and I look forward to hearing your sweet soft voice." No sooner had Christiana's flushed face had faded she blushed once more and lowered her head. It had not gone without Carver noticing. "You are... very quick to blush. I assume your..." He stopped talking for a moment, not able to bring himself to say it; after all, *If anyone should be this sweet girl's husband, it should* not *be him...* "Acel does not compliment you enough, if at all. I shall remedy that."

With a giggle, she handed him some food, and then moved closer to him a tankard of drink that remained on the table beside the bed.

"To continue… it is strange how we have spoke on many things these weeks, if only brief, yet we have avoided this topic, even though we want to know the answers. Strange. But where were we? Ah, yes. Where I found you. It is a series of events that I am pleased to say have taken my thoughts elsewhere. I thank you for that. When I discovered you, I had reason to hope once again. I am pleased my childish dreams may actually become real." Christiana's voice grew increasingly sombre which made Carver put down his plate back on the side table, and after taking a few sips from his tankard, he decided he could neither eat nor drink. "We are in Peterborough. It has now been nearly two months since I found you.

"I have taken care of you throughout that time. Gladly so. To begin with, you had woken briefly and spoke, but made no sense. You never even opened your eyes. I made sure you drank, all the while keeping you and your wounds clean. They are healing remarkably well.

"I told them that you were my cousin and only living relative I had remaining. The soldiers accepted my word. My…" she paused, no longer wanting to call him husband. If anyone, she would rather Carver have that title. "Acel… although wounded, he took pity on me and allowed me to take you into our home. Perhaps it will turn out mortally so. Acel, not you, I mean. Forgive me for thinking such things. I wish I did not." Christiana looked at Carver, hoping it would not alter his opinion of her.

"Whoa! Whoa!" he said, hurriedly drawn out, wanting to reassure her. "I do not. I mean I do, forgive you, that is." This made Christiana smile. "But more important, after how he has treated you, it is natural you want to get away. You are a good person. Do not think anything but of yourself, for I do, only what is pure and good. I better be making myself understood, my sweet one." He said firmly before smiling.

"Aye, my lord." She clasped one of his hands.

"You were saying, my sweet one." For a girl who worked hard, her hands were surprisingly smooth.

"The following morning, I was assisting in the care of Acel whilst we were set to travel back home. As an impatient man, he wanted to move when he desired and not allow anyone save his superiors and the king, new king that is, to get in his way. As I said, he was wounded. He had informed others to follow his path as he pursued some prey, as he put it, if he did not return. They had done so and found him. He had killed a few men during the route, but one had gotten away, he informed them. Although advised against travel at that particular moment, they permitted him to recover at his home. Acel's impatience had proved his undoing. Along the journey home, his wound became infected, and this led to a fever. We were brief guests at a few homes. It was at one of these, we had called for a physician. He tended to his infected wound, telling him that with prayer and a loving hand taking care of him, he would survive. We did not tell him the truth. The infection had spread. Most likely take Acel's life, but we thought best not to say. It was there the physician worked a miracle on you. I may have discovered you, but without him, you would not have survived. He told me how to attend you in order for you to live, and I thank God that He was not ready to take you before I got a chance to know how wonderful you are.

I saved you, now you may save me," Christiana said, glancing to the sky, and then Carver; she sighed pleasantly before smiling for a moment.

"But how..."

"Shh... rest some more. How I discovered you? Drink some more. Then, and only then, I will tell you. It is imperative that you do." Christiana handed Carver the tankard of drink.

She has taken care of me well, thus far. I shall do as she instructs.

Carver was not thirsty, but still drank most of whatever it was that Christiana had mixed.

A very pleasant taste. I shall ask what is in it, but later... "Thank you." He handed Christiana back the tankard.

After putting it back on the table next to the bed, she continued. "His servants were clearing the road of snow for us when we found a soldier. For whom he fought, his servants could not tell. One man recognised the sword, but I told him as similar it was, it did not belong to Acel. I am sorry to say, I lied. But rethinking the event through, I am not."

"If you need forgiveness, my sweet one, you have it, but you have nothing to be sorry about." She squeezed his hand at such reassurance.

Did she say the sword was similar, but that was a lie? I only took one sword, I think. I thought I kept my sword. No wait, I did lose it. Then... that bit is slowly coming back to me.

"You seem lost in thought. Do you need more rest?" Christiana asked, concerned.

"Oh, sorry, no. No, I am fine. A memory I nearly had forgotten was returning. Do continue." Carver was feeling somewhat tired, but was determined to hear the rest of her story.

"I am pleased. That is a good sign." Christiana smiled. "As I was saying... Acel had though about ignoring the man, once removed from the path, of course. He would never have run over any man, it would ruin the wheels." She shook her head at the thought of how Acel's mind worked. "It was at that moment I discovered something else. The sword caught my attention, but did not mean what I thought it might have. This something else, on the other hand, confirmed everything. Keeping such knowledge to myself, I told Acel and the soldiers that you were my cousin. I said that I thought you had long since passed on in battle. In truth, I have no cousins. Both my parents sadly lost siblings to one illness or another. I feigned the appropriate joy at finding you. Acel was that much drained, he cared not in probing further. The soldiers that accompanied us assumed that such a sweet looking girl would not lie about such a thing, even though chances were highly improbably at such a find."

Carver gently freed his hand that Christiana held, directing his hand to the space beside him. He ordered, "Come... sit beside me. I want to hold you."

Smiling, she walked around to the other side of the bed and sat next to him, comfortably cuddling into him. Carver put his arm around her and kissed her head. "Thank you, my lord." She felt more loved at that point, as well as any time with Carver, short as it was, than her entire time with Acel.

Christiana enjoyed him holding her so lovingly; for a few minutes, she remained silent. He, too, enjoyed holding this sweet girl, his sweet girl, he determined, and would not hurry her along with her story. He had an unfortunate feeling much worse was to come with the sadness that came across her face.

"Before the Second Battle of St. Albans and after the Battle of Wakefield something terrible occurred." The pain in her voice became apparent; her voice and body began to shake. "From what I was informed, after the success of the Lancastrians at Wakefield, an army of Englishmen from the north of the country, Welshmen, along with Scottish and French mercenaries rode towards London."

"Oh, God... have mercy upon you." Carver sighed and heavily leaned his head backwards hitting the headboard.

Christiana looked sharply at him. With tears in her eyes, but holding them back, she asked, "You know what happened because you heard or because you were there!?" Her sweet voice was more scared than angry for fear of an answer she did not want to hear.

"How did you know I had fought in the... the sword. Wait... the lock of hair. Yours. No, I was not there. But yours?" He wanted to reassure that he had no part in what his sweet girl was fast approaching in her story. Carver kissed her forehead and held her firmly. He knew she appreciated it, as much as knowing he was not among such an ill-disciplined bunch of men. *But the lock of hair was hers,* he thought. He shook his head and focussed on what she had to say for the present.

"Then as you know," she continued, not wanting to cry until she had finished. "This town is among several others along the Great North Road. As they marched south for London, they brought on great destruction towards such towns with Yorkist connections. Among the destruction that lay in their path..." She had no need to finish what she was about to say, but wanted to. "My..." she said, taking a deep breath, "my young sister, mother and father were killed. I was not informed of how they passed on, whether it was known or by choice." No longer able to hold back her tears, she trembled as she spoke. "I want to know, but on the other... do, I do n-" Christiana held onto Carver tightly and buried her head into him and allowed herself to release all her emotions. Such emotions she did not trust nor want to share with the ailing man in a room on the floor above.

Carver held her tight and caressed her hair. He felt useless at such a point. He could do nothing to alter what had happened, but wanted to make her feel safe and yet at the same time not a prisoner. She had suffered that feeling for three years. Too long. No more. If she so needed, he would hold his sweet girl all day and allow her to cry. He felt horrible hearing her so distraught, comforting her as best he could. He continued to caress her hair, allowing himself be there to hold.

Within half an hour, Christiana had fallen asleep. He could feel how at ease she had become as her unsteady pulse and breathing turned slow and tranquil while she slept. Her grip relaxed from being tight against him as if not wanting to let go to such a form of comfort to becoming at ease knowing she was well loved and protected.

Carver felt a closeness that he did not want to end, but more realistic than his sweet girl. *Acel may still recover. Unlikely as it though seemed.*

Enjoying his time with her, even if discovering some horrible news, he soon found himself so relaxed that he gave into tiredness.

Three hours had passed when, with a nudge and a kiss, Christiana woke Carver. "I need to leave. Trust that I will return at the first instant."

Slowly opening his eyes, he turned towards her and kissed her hand. "Gladly... yet impatiently."

"Nay. I will not. I shall return to you presently." She walked out of the room, only to returned half of an hour later. Carver was curious as to what she was doing, but guessed, and was correct. "I have arranged a servant to tend to him. He shall be informed that I am arranging food supplies and such." She walked around the bed, got under the sheets and leaned into him. "You will now tell me more about yourself and your family."

"Well... I am here. The end," Carver said with a mild laugh as he cuddled Christiana; she was not impressed and gave a stare to confirm it. He grimaced humorously before changing his tone. "Do not give me that look, you, my sweet girl, or you will be placed across my lap." This made her smile briefly before returning purposely to her previous countenance. "I was not serious. About a walloping, aye, I was. But now," he paused, pondering for a moment. "The most appropriate place to begin is my father's name. Humphrey. My parents seemed to like it so much or maybe my mother had. Whichever, they decided to burden me with it. I never discovered whether my father liked it. I always assumed he had. I will have to find out when we visit them."

"There you have it." Christiana could not resist interrupting. "It is not as terrible a name as you think. One of our children should be named such."

"Do not even dare suggest it. One day you may wear me down, but not yet. Until then, my hand will provide your bottom with a good walloping at the next suggestion." He spoke as firm as he could.

She felt mischievously at ease with Carver and she pushed the subject. "Then you admit it. It is only a matter of time."

He put his hand under the sheets, raised her dress, and gave as hard a smack across her bared bottom as was possible considering the angle. He caressed that beautiful bottom for a moment before continuing. "My parents are alive. They live in the Isle of Mann. They were not born there. Their story, in a way, is similar to ours in as much that this war made them want to find somewhere where they could live without the threat of it visiting, or a chance of revisiting, them.

"It is true that as far as civil wars are concerned, this one has left the majority of this island to go about its daily business unaffected. As you understand, those who want power, to control the unstable king or as now, to replace a king, want the support of the common people. Destruction on a mass scale would not gain a great deal of support.

"Sadly, as you know with your family, this was not always the case. As such, there have been occasions where destruction away from the battlefield has taken place. My parents feared this at the first signs of trouble. My father wanted to protect his family. He remembered stories from the civil war between King Stephen and his cousin, Empress Maud -or Matilda, depending on what people chose to call her- battling for the crown. That war went back and forth, when a queen or king could be so one month without a guarantee the next. Moreover, sadly with it, came much destruction throughout the land. Believing that such would occur once more, he wanted to keep his family safe. He was no longer capable of fighting as he once was. I had no desire to leave. Accepting my decision, he took my mother. Later, he would send a message informing me of where they settled. My father had accumulated enough money to travel and buy a new respectable tavern whilst still allowing me to own the one he had decided to leave. How he came to own one, I will now tell...

"He was once a loyal servant to a wealthy lord. He was a highly skilled bowman and fighter, and when the king, old Henry, Henry V, was preparing an invasion of France, my father found a place in the lord's personal retinue. My father had not seen battle, but had proved highly skilled in practice and competitions, and was more than a valuable asset to his lord. On that bleak autumn day, October 25 1415, at the Battle of Agincourt, he saved his lord's life. My father recognised him in peril, drew his sword, and came to his aid. Killing one and wounding another on that muddy, bloody and rainy day, he managed to wound another before a sword struck him. That was all his lord had needed to gain the advantage. He killed the third man in the party that planned to either capture or kill him before turning on the man that struck my father. I will put it mildly and say he killed the knight. In saving his lord's life, my father lay in agony on the ground with his right arm severed and trampled into the mud soaked field. His lord hurried him towards the baggage where he had my father attended to with haste; without haste, my father otherwise would have perished like so many of the enemy that day.

"The lord, whose employment my father was under, had with him his own physician who immediately attempted to keep my father alive. They thought it was highly unfortunate to live and yet lose his right arm. I disagree. It could have been much worse. In fact, my father was very fortunate; he was left-handed.

"Some French have complained since then about the actions taken by Henry V to kill nearly two thousand captured knights. What they need to realise is that the king had little choice. At the outset, they were outnumbered five to one. Tired from their march from Harfleur, suffering sickness and dysentery, they faced confident and fresh French. Against all odds, they managed a victory. Thanks to the longbow, the rain filled weather, a muddy field caused by a few days of more heavy rain, together with French confidence that turned into arrogance; this had led to the French's downfall.

"At one point, when victory had seemed certain, there was an attack on the baggage area. The king had got wind of the French battle plans, which favoured a rear flanking assault. They thought that this had been the earlier stages of such an action that would lead into a counter attack. My father was lucky to escape with his life, being in no fit state to fight. With this action by the French, it had doomed those captive. They were too few in number to guard not only nearly two thousand knights, but also fight off a counter attack. He ordered the captured killed. This, as you can imagine, my sweet girl, was not a popular decision. Those knights, and especially a good number, could provide an incredible ransom and make any man, in particular one who might have been struggling, very wealthy, indeed... or at least a lot better off than before. His knights refused. However, his personal bodyguard of Welsh bowman had no such feelings of chivalry towards captured knights. They knew very well that in return they would not have received such knightly treatment. He sent fifty to do the unfortunate task, and so totalled, he dispatched around two thousand captured men. Needlessly so, my sweet one, for as that day ended, a counter attack was not forthcoming. The day, as you know, was victorious for our English army. Exhausted, everyone drew a deep breath of relief. With only a few hundred killed, with perhaps as little as even one hundred, and about eight thousand French lay slain on that field, it was a day no one present would forget. They gave much praise to God that it was over, and soon they retuned home in triumph.

"For my father's service and saving his lord's life, he was granted a sum of money that would have him comfortable for the rest of his days. As a further gift of gratitude, his lord bought him a respectable tavern that would bring in a regular income."

"That is remarkable and most fortunate," Christiana remarked with admiration. "I am sorry that your father lost his arm, but in return he will remain comfortable for life." Giving Carver a squeeze, she was desperate to hear about him. His kind nature, she loved. She would not want that to change. She also enjoyed hearing tales of brave men. Honourable brave men, that was, and those that knew the meaning of a kind heart. "Now, my lord. Allow me your story."

"A pleasure. Throughout its strange twists and turns, it brought me to you.

"I was young, fit and strong. Highly skilled with both the bow and the sword, and just like my father, I was a welcomed addition in any lord's force. I was by no means wealthy, but owning a respectable tavern left to me by my father gave me enough income to purchase a horse. This would allow me to become a mounted archer. As such, my pay was higher than that of a foot archer. Archery was something I had loved since a child. I could not compete with my father, him only having one arm, but he gave me the sound advice I needed in order to improve.

"And so..." He looked down to see Christiana frown thoughtfully, "you look confused, my sweet one?"

"Are not mounted archers only used in armies of the Middle East?"

Carver laughed. "You are so adorable." He kissed her forehead, and then answered, "Those are horse archers. We dismount for battle."

"Oh... I," she said, blushing, "feel so silly."

"Do not be. If you do not know of such things, it's an easy enough err to make," Carver said, squeezing her. He then continued. "During 1455, at the age of sixteen, and battle looming, I allowed the tavern to be left in safe keeping with a trusted friend of my father.

"The Lancastrians were recruiting men in the area, and although skilled, I had doubts as to whether I wanted to go through with it. My two best friends from childhood, Glenn and Bryce were more than willing, and so we joined a small company.

It is amusing that a little later, after Wakefield, when we were celebrating, the bartender referred to us, affectionately, as the *Rainbow Warriors*. You see, we all have blue eyes, but this man was pointing out our hair colour. Glenn had red hair; Bryce, blonde; and me, brown. It would have been more appropriate if we had different eye colours, too, but still, we were also standing, without thinking, in height order. Glenn was the tallest; Bryce was a little shorter than me. We all had strong builds, but Bryce was a little broader than I, where Glenn, still solidly built, was a thinner set. Both were always good company, especially when drinking, though Glenn had an uncanny way of making us laugh under any circumstance. Although we were all skilled fighters, where I was better with the sword and bow, hand to hand, no one outmatched Bryce.

"But back to the story, my little sweet one… It would be the first battle for all three of us. Any nerves I felt were calmed in their presence.

"I mention this battle because even in defeat, I gained a victory. It also helped me to figure what I wanted. Although fighting in battles was not one of them, it is fascinating how I would find myself drawn to them.

"22 May drew closer. My friends and I thought, as well as many others, that an actual battle would never take place. We thought a negotiation similar to times in the past would take place and soon we not be needed.

"We were very wrong. Negotiations had failed and the battle commenced at around ten in the morning. The Yorkist attack was sudden. It caught us all off guard. They simultaneously attacked the town gates on Sopwell Lane and Shropshire Lane. My friends and I were defending the gate at Sopwell Lane. Whilst we were doing well in defending our position, unbeknown to us at the time, Warwick had managed to pass in between and burst into the market place, where opposite was the king's position in the main street. Warwick shattered the Lancastrian line in two. That was it. The battle was soon lost. Fearing a rear attack, men all around us at the gate broke line and fled. We had no choice but to do the same. The Yorkists would enter through the unmanned gates.

"A Lancastrian force tried to rally around the king, but it was only a brave effort. An arrow attack at short range proved overwhelming. The king was wounded in the neck. Until then you could find him seated in silence under a tree. The fighting around did not last long. My friends and I managed to flee to a building where we hid as the Yorkist surrounded the abandoned king. He managed to calm them with relative ease. The Yorkists led him away where York asked for forgiveness. In a few months, as you know, he would rule England as Protector and Defender of the Land.

"I became a hero through my next actions. There was heavy looting after the Yorkist victory, which gave me the opportunity I needed. Hiding away near the abbey, I was able to find several cowls. I handed them to my friends and a few others. I refused to take one for myself and took my chances following a similar route to my friends. They had no idea I was planning to refuse one for myself. I let them go on ahead and then chose a different path to escape.

"This act of bravery, allowing the chance for several others to escape with greater ease whilst refusing to safe guard my own, gained the admiration of my town, and of course the women. Even in defeat, I gained a victory."

Looking up at Carver with admiration, she asked, "Why did you refuse to take the disguise?"

"Well, my sweet one. If anyone wanted to know the tale,

and there were many a willing ear in my tavern, I would inform them that I wanted to safe guard the lives of as many as possible, most importantly my friends. Of course, in actuality there was more to it than that. Safe guard the lives of my friends, of course. And if I could help any other, then I welcomed that, too. There was a little more to it than that. I knew that if I had put on the cowl... I would not have wanted to remove it. As you see, my sweet one. Not brave at all.

"Somerset, knowing the battle was lost, the man whom York would replace, made his final charge from his refuge in the Castle Inn with a few of his retainers after Lord Clifford, with Harrington and Percy along with other knights outside were slain, killed four before being felled by an axe. That is braver than I. A slight difference; Somerset had no choice. I, as a commoner, might have been spared if discovered. I did not want to take that chance."

Not brave! These words irritated her. Before she addressed this issue, one other thing would come first. Christiana sat up and spoke fast. "It is good you did not. For both our sakes. The cowl, I mean. You must not think like that again. Loving God, I can understand. But you have a duty to me. Well, I hope not duty. You know what I am saying. I hope you know what I am... I..."

"Shh... calm yourself, my little sweet one. I am not going to become a monk. I have grown since then and know what I want. I want a peaceful life, but want with it a girl, and one that understands me. I believe that is you."

Christiana sighed with much relief. "I am very glad to hear that. I do, my lord. I panicked. Forgive me. I want to share that life with you. You are a brave warrior, in spite of your own opinion. You may wallop my bottom, but I will not have you saying you are not brave. Still, what is more endearing is that I love you more for your ability to fight, yet with it, deep inside is a peaceful soul."

"I am very happy you feel that way, my sweet one," Carver said, kissing her forehead. He then raised her chin with his forefinger and kissed her tiny nose; followed by gently kissing her lips. He caressed her cheek, and allowed her to lean into him.

A tingle of joy rushed through her. It was only a few hours before when she was feeling upset at talking about her family, but Carver had a way of making her feel so happy. She cuddled into him, and asked, "Please, my lord. Please continue."

He took a deep breath. "Well... until times recent I spent most my time running the day to day affairs of my tavern. I kept in contact with my parents twice yearly. Owning my own business and dealing with out of control drunkards made me popular, further still, with the women. None cared about my peaceful desires, and so I went along with the flow. I would drink with my friends and have fun with the women. Life seemed fine. I had little of which to give cause for complaint.

"During 1459, as you know, my sweet one, the situation disintegrated once more into civil war. With battles fought during 1459 and 1460, lords were seeking recruits, and one in particular came to my town and tavern. My friends were willing to fight again. We were enjoying the night with a good drink, and volunteered once more to be apart of a small company.

"I had experienced defeat and it would not be long before I would feel the elation of victory at Wakefield. I still practiced with my friends with archery and the sword. We remained skilled fighters, just not professionals. I once again left charge of my tavern in safekeeping, this time to the son of the man that I entrusted before. As 1460 neared its end, a battle was certain. My friends and I enjoyed

Christmas. We were in good spirits for the battle to come... 31 December."

"Ah... Acel had fought in that battle," she mentioned, fascinated.

"Was he? Really? And we only came face to face a few months later."

"He told me a little about the battle and how he was fortunate to survive. He thought my lock of hair that he carried with him, hoping my angelic features would bring him luck, was what brought on this fortune. He was surprised he had never thought of it before, and as a result, he was very kind to me. This did not last long. The resentment of not being able to provide him with a child brought old feelings back. He never once considered the problem was his; after all, it was he who slept with whomever he pleased." Christiana felt increasingly angered.

Caressing her, he reassured, "It will be fine. As things fall into place, you will soon discover how I came to have your locket in my possession. Though, my sweet one, I do believe you know. But still, perhaps Acel was right. It did, after all, provide *me* with much fortune."

She smiled. "I look forward to hearing of your confrontation." She kissed his chest and leaned back into him.

"I have been fortunate to experience victory in defeat and then the relief and joy of genuine victory. We all received injuries, my friends more so than I. Such wounds prevented them from joining me at Towton. I do praise God for that. A few days later, we got together and had a good drink to celebrate, equally for surviving as much as the victory itself.

"The snow that fell after the battle was an experience. It covered the dead like a blanket. The horrors of battle found itself covered for the night.

"We lived in a town with Lancastrian ties, and so naturally we joined this army. I would not fight against the king, no matter how awfully advised, as had occurred in the past. His peaceful nature, I admired. He abhorred violence, was pious, chose simple dress for someone of his stature, founded universities, and was kind and generous to those he loved. Perhaps not suited for the world we live in. He was too easily led or controlled, thus prone to poor advice. This unfortunately, as we all discovered, led to trouble and unpopularity across parts of the land.

"I do not dislike the new king; apart from he would have had me killed at Towton. Then again, after what happened at Wakefield, it is not surprising."

Christiana had a little knowledge of what occurred, but was enjoying him tell the story and did not want to have him rush through too swiftly. She would enjoy hearing it in more detail. *That is if he would allow it at a later date,* she thought.

"The sons of some of those killed at the Battle of St. Albans were present. This did not bode well for the captured sons of those who had once slain their parents. In revenge, Lord Clifford, who had captured Edmund, Earl of Rutland, and Sir Robert Aspell, summarily executed both for the killing of his father, who had fell outside the Castle Inn all those years back.

"With his father, Edward of York, killed in battle at Wakefield, and Edmund, his seventeen year old brother executed soon after, with both their heads put upon spikes on Micklegate Bar, the new Duke of York, eighteen year old Edward, was in no mood for remorse. Both sides stated they neither wanted nor would give any quarter in order to settle the matter once and for all... and thus set the scene for such an 'orrendous battle."

"It was said the river ran with blood for days after the Towton; a possible five-and-twenty to thirty thousand killed. Injured as you were, you would not have known this... I did not know what to believe. So many," Christiana said stunned, yet wanted to inform Carver. This number, indeed, had shocked her.

"I did not know of that," Carver responded, equally shocked, but not surprised. "The battle had lasted all day. The route lasted all night and, I have no doubt, into the morning. The latter, I assume.

"It began that cold day, 29 March 1461. We, the Lancastrian army began strategically well. We were first onto the field, holding the advantage of height on the plateau; the Cock Beck River protected our right flank.

"That grey and bitter morning began well. Snow began to fall and blow into the faces of the Yorkist army.

"That soon changed. As our armies were forming, the weather had swung its directions, and as the snow began to fall even heavier, blowing straight in our faces, we could see not a thing. This caused panic.

"Every archer wants to be the first to fire a volley. We are, after all, the sons and grandsons of those archers who caused such havoc against the French at Agincourt. There were some soldiers present, I heard, that had actually fought at Agincourt. This time, however, instead of the French, it was against our own countrymen. We could fire ten to fifteen arrows a minute. Whoever succeeded in firing first had the advantage. I would have felt better if my two best friends were with me, until that is, the Yorkists under cover of the snow, crept closer and let loose the first volley.

"It was at that moment, I became glad they had not been present. Men to the left and right of me began to fall as a rain of arrows struck into them. Some tried to fire back only to have themselves felled, too, by the storm of arrows. I used my shield for cover..."

"My lord... Um, sorry to interrupt. I was told by... you know... that your arrows were falling, due to the wind, much short of their targets. When the Yorkist archers had nearly spent their arrows, they simply picked up yours from the ground and fired them back... sorry," she said, not wanting to look at him.

"Do not be. None of this is your fault," he said with a sigh. "But it does explain why the sky felt a mix of snow and arrows. I tried to fire when I thought it best. Not easy. As men fell all around, their screams combined with the weather, all added to confusion. So many were dead around me... then blank... for what was, I assume, a few hours. Maybe more.

"An arrow wounded me in the side of my right leg. I felt light-headed and confused. I scooped a handful of snow and placed it gratefully in my in my mouth to aid hydration. I snapped the arrow, but kept the arrowhead and part of the arrow imbedded. I did not want to risk removing it.

"I gazed at what I could see of the battle ahead of me. We had advanced with pole, sword and axe. I could barely move. Whilst I gathered strength, I witnessed a sight I never thought possible. I remained, barely able to move, unnoticed among so many dead. My hearing had temporarily diminished, but could hear the sounds of battle; remembering the sound of a barrage of arrows through the air; to now hearing sword crashing against sword, pole or axe, or against shield or armour; screams of men in pain or shouting commands or taunts. With my momentary loss of hearing, at first I could not tell one from another. As I watched the battle unfold, my hearing slowly returned to me, though still not as clear as it is now. The battle seemed to sway back and forth; the advantage against the Yorkists, they being fewer, not by much mind you, in number. The battle had clearly gone on for hours. At this time, there were some knights, in particular with heavy armour, resting before going back into the fray. So much was the slaughter of men that several times both sides had to stop fighting and pull back their dead to clear space, and then fight once more. I had not seen anything like this before. I was stunned. Slowly gaining movement, I made my way through the snow and piles of bodies. The smell of sweat, blood and... well, I feel I should not go into too great a detail. I do not believe it is suitable for such a sweet girl's ear. The air smelled as you might imagine for a battle on such a scale."

"Erm... Well, I do not want to hear too gory a detail, but I do enjoy tales of kind, brave men, such as you, my kind sir. But to let you know, I was informed that the soon to become king, Edward IV, rode up and down his line, joining the fight wherever he saw it weaken. This gave strength to his men as he fought beside them. Before hand, he gave a speech allowing any man who wanted to leave to do so. But once battle had begun, any man deserting would be considered a traitor," she added.

"That would explain their continued spirit. More so with the arrival of what I assumed were re-enforcements from the Yorkist side, they gradually gained the momentum. In time, how long of which I cannot say, the Lancastrian line broke and fled, and what would be an even greater slaughter in what was once a protected flank became a river that would either drown or slow down and ultimately cause so much more slaughter than was already on the field. I made my way slowly back to try escaping through the woods.

"It was the nobles that were sought and not the commoners, but with such a route, nobody would halt this slaughter.

"Whilst I tried to make my slow escape, I believe someone with excellent eyes had seen a wounded prey. He decided to peruse him alone. Confident with victory, he wanted to savour the moment of this pursuit. I could hear his galloping horse and tried to move faster. I was fortunate in receiving wounds that caused me to fall down and become unconscious so early in the battle. Otherwise, I may not have had the advantage denied to so many at that moment.

"He approached; I could hear the sound of his horse crushing the snow beneath its hooves not far behind. He called out to me. I nearly ignored him, but if I ran, I was no more. My only remaining option was to turn and fight. I had lost my armoured helmet at a point in which I cannot remember; this proved most unfortunate. He played with me as he rode around the trees. He knew I could not outrun him. As he charged towards me, I discovered to my alarm that I was too weak to swing my sword. Before I knew it, he had swung his sword and knocked mine out of my hands causing it to fly up in the air, and I, onto my back."

Although she knew how it must have ended, Christiana felt her nerves shaking as Carver detailed his fight with her... with Acel.

"He rode towards me once more, striking his sword down the side of my face and knocking me back to the ground. For a moment, I lost consciousness, but only for a moment. I tried to get up. The cold prevented me from feeling the pain I should have felt. Perhaps the blood pumping through me prevented such. That blood was escaping through the wound in my face.

"He dismounted and removed his helmet. His dark eyes and brownish hair turned black due to sweat with his chiselled features made him appear highly menacing. I will admit that he was to me, so weakened a state I was in. He was also a little taller than I... or perhaps it was that I could no longer stand as upright as usual.

He was confident enough to take his time, so certain he was that I was finished. Slowly walking towards me, taunting me, he pointed his sword in my direction. I stood breathless, trying to remain upright. I was determined not to hold my newly formed wound, in spite of feeling the blood pour down my face and gradually feeling its pain.

"He looked to the sky with a chortle. That was all I could stand from this arrogant swine. I charged him. Unfortunately, my movement was not as swift as it should; what it normally would were I at my usual health. He saw it coming and sliced at my arm, forcing me to stumble back. Involuntary, I held my arm.

"He approached and spoke; 'Now you are in peril!'... What else could I do but feign even greater weakness for a moment, which did not take a lot of effort. 'I am bored with you,' he finished off. 'Not even a challenge.'

"He raised his sword, intending to strike it across my body. That was my moment. I could not stand well, but on the ground, I was very much capable of fighting, if only barely.

"I charged him once again. This time, thankfully, I was more successful. The sword fell from his hands as we fell onto the snow-covered ground. I slammed my head into his face, followed immediately with a hammer punch. I needed to take the momentum whilst he was stunned. My burst of energy had slumped, and so very much weakened was I, it was a slow process unleashing my dagger from its sheath. He began to rouse, no doubt aiming to wrestle me off him. He would still have much more strength than I, for that moment, and so I struck the blade into the nearest body part. I smashed it as hard as possible, piercing his armour, into his left thigh. He grabbed hold of me as he screamed out. Before he could do anything else, I slammed my head into him once more and twisted the dagger, hearing him scream louder as I wrenched it from him, the force causing me to fall on my side for a few seconds; I then fell flat on my back, breathless.

"I wanted to stay put, but knew that would be a clear mistake. The trees gave a sense of peace that was not present that day. I was unable to appreciate the view for long. I slowly began to move.

"I decided to leave him to bleed to death. For taunting me, he deserved that. I noticed a lock of hair beside him. It must have fallen from his possession. I clutched it and moved as fast as I could.

"I remember little as I became more and more weary... I picked up a sword before I fled, thinking it were mine. As I have learned, it was not. Still, I give praise to God for you; you were soon to discover me."

Christiana could not speak, only look up at Carver with wide eyes. She felt much respect and admiration for him. If time were convenient, she would have leapt on him with passion. Words could not leave her mouth. She mimed, 'I love you.'

If he had a little more strength, Carver would have done the same. "With out any doubt, my sweet girl, I love you, too." He had not felt such for any girl before.

"I am thirsty, my lord," she said, sitting up. "Hungry as well. I will make you some food. I would rather something else, as I am sure you do... we shall find time for that. For now, you need your strength to recover. I will make us something to eat." She closed her eyes, pretended it was only them two in her home for the moment, leaned towards Carver, and gave him a long and sensual kiss.

"Beautiful, my sweet little one... as to be expected. I look forward to when we are certain of alone time and greater privacy where, and with pleasure, I can take my time in pleasing you. That includes a longing to have you across my lap. Your beautiful bottom is in great a need of becoming bared for my hand to both gently caress and be firmly applied," he said before giving her a smile.

Christiana noticed how he kept making her blush. She ordered, "You stay there."

"I have no where to go... besides, I would not dare," Carver said as he winked. He then smacked her bottom as she got off the bed and left the room.

Nearly a week had passed before Carver and Christiana were able to spend the time together that they had wanted. Acel had become gravely ill; it was either kill or cure. For the time being, there was no certainty as to which.

Carver was feeling a lot better and able to walk freely around Christiana's home and garden. He enjoyed the carefree emotions that filled him. Since it may not last for much longer, he savoured this time whilst it was available. The servants were living in a separate area of the household. Christiana ordered them to, for the time being, stay away from where Carver or Acel were resting. Giving them less work, this pleased them. As for Christiana, it gave her the privacy that she desired. Almost.

It was a beautiful day. Carver lay on the grassy slope in the garden waiting for Christiana. He felt so much at ease and at peace. He could not wait for Acel to leave this world, praying for forgiveness at such a thought. He mused whilst gazing at the clouds in the bright sky, *God knew the man that was Acel; the manner he treated women and those of humble origins.*

Time passed pleasantly. *A beautiful day. I would love to enjoy it with Christiana. She is taking a long time.*

Carver knew that Acel could keep her detained for a while, and as Christiana had explained, Acel was never so kind and gentle as he was at such a time. If he were to make a full recovery, Carver knew for certain it would not take long before he became the man he once was, and that would lead only to misery. *I hope she calculates the same.*

Carver decided on another walk around the huge garden, this time paying more attention to the flowers and hedges.

I would love to own such as this. On a day like today, it would be perfect for Christiana and me.

It felt like another world; clean, peaceful, and on a beautiful day with the sounds of the birds, it was almost indescribable. He found the words... *with my little sweet one, Christiana... Bliss.*

She is taking an awful long time. Perhaps Acel was no longer in this world.

There was only one way to know what was detaining his sweet girl. Carver walked back inside Christiana's home and began a search.

Carver did not want to shout for her in case Acel was asleep; if he was, Carver had no desire to wake him. There was no desire for Acel to consume even more of her time.

It was a huge household, and so where to start? It was obvious, but Carver decided to walk towards his room in case she was there. That seemed unlikely; they had arranged to meet outside. Carver had not walked near where Acel was resting, but had to reassure himself that Acel was not detaining her longer than at any other time.

With a creeping walk to the top of the square revolving staircase and whispering his sweet girl's name, he wondered strangely what would happen if Acel had recovered, and even more peculiar, decided to take a walk. There was an eerie silence, apart from the creaking of the floorboards as Carver crept.

He made a slow and careful walk, passing several rooms, which took him to a point that would lead to a corridor; the corridor led to the master room. This was Acel's place of rest and recovery.

Carver came close to the door. It was odd to find it open.

He could not hear any voices. This puzzled him further. It was not a good idea to whisper for Christiana in case Acel was awake. There was little Acel was capable of doing in such a condition. It mattered not. Carver did not wish to be tempted to finish what he had nearly accomplished on the battlefield.

In time, God shall take him.

Carver crouched in order to be out of sight when he peaked into the room, if Acel were awake, *Or even alive for that matter.*

The moment Carver was about to peer into the room, he heard Christiana.

It sounds like... no, wait, she is *weeping. Acel must have departed. But why would she cry?*

Carver stood and walked into the room.

Acel was alive, if only barely. To Carver's relief, he was not awake. Carver walked carefully towards Christiana and was about to query her emotional state when he saw a dagger in her hand. Relief turned to shock, and controlling a sudden rush of panic, Carver almost broke into a dash as he grabbed Christiana and removed the dagger from her hand.

Carver had not imagined he could feel so furious with his sweet girl. The moment he removed the dagger from her possession, he grabbed her other hand and pulled her along. Placing the dagger in a near by drawer, he continued to walk out of the room.

Closing the door as quietly as he could was not at all made easy bearing in mind his mood. He scolded, "You are in more trouble than you can imagine, my girl!" He moved Christiana in front of him, and as they walked along the corridor, no longer concerned with keeping quiet, his hand smacked across her bottom several times. "You wait until I have you downstairs. I shall grant you a reason to weep!"

"I did it for us. He may recover," she said, sobbing.

Carver had passed in front of Christiana and was dragging her by the hand down the stairs. "You once told me not to act in haste. I cannot believe you would think we could get away with doing such a thing." He stopped at the bottom of the staircase. "I believe that the empty barn will provide the desired privacy from that *Ass'* ear, will it not?" he asked.

"Yes, my lord. It shall." The consequences of what she had just attempted dawned upon her. She felt very much ashamed of herself. She stopped sobbing, and wiping her eyes dry with her free hand. "I am so sorry, my lord. My bottom deserves everything you are bound to give. I feel so ashamed. So much so, I feel I need punishing in front of the servants to show your place and mine. They need not know what I have done, but..."

"Shh," Carver insisted. Christiana's apology was enough to calm Carver somewhat. He was still very much angry at how reckless she had behaved. He walked her to the empty barn. "I shall speak with you in a moment."

She obeyed and remained silent. When they entered, Carver sat on the edge of a large bale of hay. Although her punishment was, she knew, well deserved, Christiana was very nervous and almost could not bring herself to lay herself over his lap. Her delayed reaction angered Carver further. He smacked her bottom hard for it. He scolded, "Do not make it worse!"

"Aye, sir. Sorry." Christiana placed her hands on his thighs, and carefully bent herself over his lap.

Carver altered her position slightly. "Unless it is of high importance, I assume none of your servants will enter this area." He held one hand firmly on her waist; the other began smacking her bottom. "If they do... I will simply inform them that my *cousin* was in need of discipline. They would not question that." He attempted to calm his breathing, but knew what would help relieve his anger and frustration, and he was doing just that, one cheek at a time.

"Ah! Ah! Ow! Ow! Ah! Owww!"

"I am pleased this is having an effect on you, my girl." The light dress that Christiana wore did not provide much protection. Feeling every hard whack, she originally wanted to grip Carver's hose, but settled with clutching his calf instead, which turned out to be a better idea; she tried not to kick, but this was not an easy task and could not resist raising or scissor kicking her legs. "Do you even know how close you came to ruining any chance we had of happily being together? Do you!?"

"Ow! Ow! Ow! Ow! Aye, A-Ow! I realise-Ow! How-Ow! Foolish I was...Ah! Ow!" Christiana found it difficult to talk since every time she tried, Carver's hand interrupted, walloping her bottom. Her attempts to apologise turned into cries of pain.

Christiana, though not meaning to, raised her legs so they bent.

"You will stop that. Kicking your legs I can allow, my girl, but not that. They get in the way."

"Ow! Ow! For-Ow! Give... Forgive me-Ow! I cannot-Ow! Help it, my lord-Ow! Ow!"

Carver halted and pulled back Christiana's dress and revealed a beautiful bare bottom that shone a delicate pink. "You do not want me to break off a branch from one of those trees in the garden and whack you with that, do you?"

"No, No please. I will attempt against it, my lord," she answered him desperately. *Your hand is enough*, she thought. She took a deep breath, but was unable to breathe steadily with Carver walloping her now, bare bottom.

"It appears that God will take your," he paused, wanting to strike himself for what he nearly had said, "Acel away from us. It shall not be you." Christiana's bottom was beginning to glow as Carver's hand smacked into each cheek, much harder than Christiana ever imagined. "I want you to remain as pure as you are at this moment. Granted, you have behaved poorly. Nevertheless, you are still pure, the way I view things."

"Aye, my lord-Ow! Ow!" Christiana began to sob as her bottom increasingly felt the heated sting. Her legs kicked frantically.

"I know you are learning your lesson, my sweet girl, even before I took you over my lap. We both know it was still warranted."

Christiana's bottom was gradually turning a crimson red. She had felt pain like this before when Acel had beaten her; however, this time was different. As painful as it was, she could differentiate the two. Carver delivered his hand with love, and that made all the difference; putting her over his lap helped with that, too. It felt more intimate.

Besides... it was, after all, my idea in the first place. Even if it had not been, I am still in need of having my bottom warmed, she thought.

Tears streaming from her eyes, she grew weaker with every wallop. Although wanting this, and not finding it very pleasant, she would want more.

Letting go of Carver's calf, she dangled, crying helplessly over his lap. With every wallop and with every tear that fell down her face, she felt relief from her foolishness.

Carver could tell she had had enough. He stopped and caressed her bottom. He had never treated a girl like this before. No longer feeling angry with her, he began to feel he had perhaps overreacted. That was until he heard a sobbing, sorry girl softly speak. "Thank you, my lord. I am sorry. I will not behave in such a manner again. I promise."

He allowed her to stand and admired how adorable she looked as she hopped around, rubbing her bottom. "I am sorry, too, my sweet girl. But do let it be known, I shall not hesitate in doing so again when next you misbehave." He had felt much relief in disciplining her. It would serve them both well in future if ever a need to clear the air.

Continuing to rub her bottom, Christiana turned and looked at him. "Do not apologise for doing what was in my best interest and for my own good. I know you love me and had done so out of love. If anyone is to apologise it will be myself." She grudgingly stopped rubbing her bottom, but wanted to do what she was about to do.

"Very wise you are, my sweet girl." Carver was about to tell her to sit on his lap. Still feeling a twinge from his healed wound, he knew that he could cope with her tiny weight. As he was about to speak, she walked fast towards him and sat on his lap, throwing her arms around him. She kissed his lips with delight; knocking him off balance due to her swiftness, they both fell into the stack of hay that was to the back of Carver.

"Oof!" He felt dazed for a moment; recovering a few seconds later, he whacked Christiana's bottom. "Thank you for that, little one. I am glad this hay was behind us or I may have had to give your bottom another good walloping," he said, laughing. He kissed her.

"Ow! Ah, yes. Sorry, my lord," she grimaced, but noticing his smile reassured her that she was not in trouble.

Carver shifted some hay behind him and used it to rest his head. He held her warmly. Christiana happily rested her head on his chest. "May I request that you rub my bottom, my lord? I deserve to feel the sting as a part of the punishment, but it does sting something fierce," she whined in an adorable manner.

"Aye. I can do that, my little sweet one. You have learned your lesson and therefore no further punishment is needed." Carver put his hand up her dress and began rubbing her bottom.

Christiana sighed with relief and closed her eyes; she relaxed. "Thank you, my lord."

"In time, my girl, we will be free from this island and to another. Since we do not know when this war will end, or even restart once it has, if it ever does, it is best we leave. It is true that compared to previous civil wars, this has left much of the country untouched apart from the battlefields. Of course, those in power wanting public support will not want to decimate town after town. Unfortunately, as you have sadly experienced, my sweet girl, there was the rare time when such thinking, by a few, was not adhered to."

Carver got up and carried Christiana into the garden. She felt even more in love with him after lovingly taking her over his lap... and now into his arms. She held her arms around his neck and leaned her head into him. "Where would we go?" she asked. "Money will not be an issue when Acel passes. He has no family either. Therefore, all he owns shall pass to me."

Carver sat in one of the large garden chairs and held Christiana on his lap; she continued to lean into him. "I never asked, but how much does he own."

"Four estates. He enjoys journeying to each for particular months of the year."

Carver's mouth opened with surprise. "That... is a lot more than I originally thought." Unable to speak, he paused for a minute. He attempted a few times and failed. Eventually, he found the words for which he was searching. She wisely allowed the thought of such money to register in his mind, enjoying her time cuddling into him. "It may take a while to sell them, unless you know of anyone. But to answer your question, sweet one. How is your Manx?"

Christiana was unable to answer. Confused, she asked, "I beg your pardon? My M-what? If you were any other man, I would consider that a highly rude question. It sounds like such."

Carver laughed, "You are too cute, my little sweet one."

"I am glad you find yourself amused by my not knowing," she sulked, embarrassed. "I feel a dim-wit."

Carver felt chagrined for upsetting his little sweet one. "Do not, my sweet girl. If you do not know then you do not know. I shall teach you. Or, in this case, learn together. I find you cute, but you are not unintelligent. You fast learned how to take care of me, after all. You ever think that way of yourself again, and your bottom, how it feels now, shall be felt tenfold. Do I make myself clear?" he asked, firmly.

"Yes, my lord. Thank you." She smiled.

"In fact." He edged himself forward and swiftly turned his little sweet one over his lap. He began smacking her bottom.

With her bottom still very much sore, she instantly burst into tears. "Oww! Ow! Ow! Ow! What-Ow! Is tha-Ow! ... that-Ow! for?" No sooner had she asked this question, Carver stopped; she lay helplessly over his lap, weeping.

"I am smacking your bottom for even thinking you are anything but intelligent. I want to make it very clear to you that you are."

"You are, my lord, I am sorry. I-nooo!" she cried, desperately, as he lifted her dress back. Her bottom was already well-punished, appearing remarkable adorable to Carver's eyes.

As Carver began walloping her well-punished bare bottom, he noticed how the smacking sound filled the air rather pleasantly.

Christiana wriggled a little with discomfort, but tried remaining still. She wanted to cry a lot louder, but was mortified at the thought of adding to the chances of attracting any attention. Her face turned bright red from just thinking of anyone interrupting them. She agreed, even though Carver had asked no question at this point. "Yes-Ow! Ow! Ow! I will behave, my-Ow! My lord. I-Ow! Ow! am intel-Ow! …tel-Ow! Intelli-Ow! Clever-Ow!"

Still smacking her bottom, Carver spoke softly but firm. "I am very glad to hear that, my girl. It is highly fortunate that no one has heard us." He stopped and allowed Christiana to sob away whilst he rubbed very sore and stinging bottom. "I shall stop and rub your poor bottom. I know you have learned your lesson. Good girl." He then kissed each cheek. "Such a beautiful bottom."

"Thank you, my lord, for punishing me and for the compliment. I almost feel unworthy of such praise. But," she quickly rushed out, not wanting more a sore and stinging bottom, for now, "I am, I am, I am. I know I am, my lord. Thank you. I am not familiar with paying compliments myself, but you mean so much to me. You truly do, my love." Not sobbing as much, she felt relief from the sting as Carver rubbed her bottom. She almost cared not if anyone saw them. She was over her man's lap after receiving some much-needed discipline. No one would think any less of her. *I deserved it, after all,* she thought.

No one interrupted them.

"But to answer you, my little sweet one," he said as he rubbed a deeply reddened, beautiful bottom. "Manx. It is a language spoken on the Isle of Mann, which if you were not certain, my sweet one, is located in the Irish Sea between Britain and Ireland, where the English-Scottish border be. They speak the same language as us, but as we have our old languages, they have one, too. Manx. I shall enjoy learning this language with you, if you so choose. Not necessary, but I would like to."

Christiana sniffed. "I would like that, too, my lord." She

found herself lifted as Carver sat her on his lap. He leaned her into him, with one hand still rubbing her heated bottom.

"Comfortable?" he asked.

"Yes, my lord," she said, smiling as she cuddled into him, her tears drying out.

Apart from the sound of the birds, there was a pleasant and peaceful silence for the following several minutes, both feeling calmed once more, feeling ever so close to one another due to him disciplining her.

Carver then spoke. "Since my parents live there, that is an advantage, as they are now familiar with the land. It would be good to see them financially secure. Even though they enjoy their tavern, I would like to see them have someone else do most of the hard work. I am confident that you will like them."

"I would like to meet them," Christiana said, feeling very happy. She then paused for thought. "On a different note, there has been something on my mind. Privacy. I have never enjoyed servants around. In large estates such as these, they are a must. Yet, considering how I wish you to treat me, I do not want anyone knowing. I want the freedom for my bottom to receive your hand at any time or place around our home." Christiana shifted her position a little. She was enjoying Carver hold her on his lap, especially after him disciplining her, but her bottom was still very much tender. "I know of whom to speak with regards to selling the estates. Nonetheless, you will need to deal with such matters in my place. And purchase the finest clothing that you desire."

Carver laughed. "Ah, aye. I am in need of such. I do not feel comfortable wearing Acel's clothes. Though, it is an additional fine thought, I shall admit, in the short term."

"I would like to provide those servants each with a large amount, in a way of gratitude for their services. I know

Acel would say," Christiana cleared her throat and impersonated his voice with an exaggerated movement of her head. "*'They aught to have gratitude towards us... for their employment. Otherwise, such would be nothing but filth on the streets! More so than what they are at present!'*" She giggled joyfully at mocking Acel.

Carver laughed louder than he expected. She sounded so cute. "From what I remember, ye have accomplished a fine performance. Whilst we wait for his passing, with all he put you through, mocking is exactly what is deserved of your..." He paused for thought.

"Gaoler."

"Aye. Very well put, my little sweet one," he agreed.

"That is additionally the reason why I want to reward the service of my servants. That is something Acel would strongly oppose. With so much money, we can live extremely well. So much so, I am not even certain what to do with it." She thought for a moment, and then said, "Aye, I nearly forgot to finish. Back to the issue of privacy, I am happy to cook for us unless we host larger gathering such as at Christmas or similar. With regards to washing, cleaning and other tasks, I guess we would need them after all," she said, disappointed.

Carver contemplated the possibilities for a minute. "Well, with a wealthy home that is nay the size of these, I foresee a problem not. Most likely, we can have built a small living area away from our home; enough for privacy and still close enough to call upon them when there is a need. I know little of wealthy homes, but am sure we can arrange thus."

"Arrange soon, I hope."

Caressing her back, Carver reassured her, "We will. Maintain those hopeful thoughts. They will come to fruition. Myself, I would like to one day own many taverns.

Even have my friends be each in the care of such."

"I have no doubt you will, my lord. I was thinking of something you told me. After telling me about your first battle and gaining a victory in defeat. It is similar to now. In defeat, my love, you have gained two victories." Carver knew what Christiana was about to say, but allowed her to finish. In truth, he wanted to hear it. "One was against Acel; the other, though different, and if truth be told, with ease... was me." She smiled, looking at Carver adoringly. She kissed him.

"By far my most satisfying victory, my little sweet one." He kissed her forehead.

The weather shone bright as Carver and Christiana relaxed and held one another. They had planned to ride together. Both had been looking forward to doing so when Carver was well enough.

"My bottom will be ever so sore when we return from our ride," she realised, wincing.

Carver laughed. "Aye, 'tis true." He decided to tease his little sweet one. "If you would rather, we can postpone it for another day."

Seriously responding, she responded, "I've waited long enough. A sore bottom is what I deserve. I have also deserved the pleasure of riding with you, my lord." Christiana got up from his lap. "I will not keep waiting for long. But I need to change into something more appropriate."

"I thought you would say that. I will watch you. After all, I have deserved that." He gave her a wink. "We both deserve something else that we shall do when we take a pause in riding; oh, how that is long overdue." Christiana giggled at his gaze to the side and exaggerated sigh. "Your servants can tend to him for now. They shall understand your need for a rest from him." He tapped her bottom. "Come now. Hurry yourself along."

Christiana smiled and obeyed.

As they rode, Christiana sitting in front of Carver, they both felt free for the first time since childhood. The speed of their horse aided in a euphoria that flowed within them; neither experienced before nor could have imagined.

Some distance away, the situation was much different. Acel had passed on in his sleep; a more merciful fate than he had granted others without care.

Several months would pass before Carver and Christiana finally sold all of her inherited properties.
Soon after, they would succeed in their journey to the Isle of Mann; fulfil their discussed plans, and live a peaceful and happy life - This is their future.

For the present, and not aware of Acel's passing, they enjoyed this taste of freedom and true alone time, relishing every second, not knowing how many times they would have such a chance for the foreseeable future.
Carver would soon share in financial security, and with their planned move to where the war was most unlikely to visit, he did not have to fight again. Most important, he had found the girl he had always wanted and was very much in love. More than he had ever thought possible. The country air had never smelled so sweet.
For Christiana, she had found a kind of security she had not known before. She felt safe and loved, and was deeply in love with Carver. She would experience and share in life something she had for so long wanted and not received. A cool breeze that drifted across felt more refreshing than ever before.

A Tennis Brat
~Brat No. 5: Jane – along with Hannah~

For a woman, Jane was of average height, but by no means an average girl, in both appearance and personality. She had large hazel eyes, which depending on her mood, were as cute as they were intimidating. Her long brown hair was in its own class of elegance. For practical reasons as well as making her look extremely cute and a touch more youthful, whenever on the tennis court, she always tied her hair into pigtails. Some players unwisely took her appearance as a sign of weakness, underestimating her ability; opponents with such an idiotic mindset soon learned otherwise.

Jim had noticed that her natural beauty matched her attitude towards hard work. The results of this were an athletic build combined with remarkable tennis skills.

Jim had been coaching the twenty-one-year old for nearly three years. Within those years, he had noticed Jane's well being and behaviour match that of her performance, improving year after year; from a teenage girl in need of affection and an outlet for her aggressive behaviour to a disciplined and well-mannered young lady... most of the time. Occasionally, her old self would emerge; she even knew herself it needed addressing.

This was not the case when she first thought about using tennis to counter her aggressive tendencies. Now, Jane would not like to imagine her life now without it, nor for that matter something else.

*

Orphaned when she was only a toddler, Jane grew up in an orphanage. Most of the girls there seemed very happy and well adjusted. On the other side of the coin, Jane harboured resentment at not being able to feel part of a family unit; a proper unit, she used to dream as a child. There was something missing, and although she was cared for, in the back of her mind, she felt unloved. It was something she would not openly admit, but had made her very unhappy.

Her teachers sensed something was wrong, of which a few had made an effort to find out what was on her troubled mind; never would she open up and tell them. Other teachers had dismissed her as a troublemaker, even when it was clear she was the aggrieved party.

It was not often that Jane had gotten into fights, but when someone tried to take advantage of her quiet nature, she soon proved it was a huge mistake on their part. Her ability to fight well, always standing her ground was, after all, the problem; some teachers looked upon her as the source of trouble, rather than someone who, unfortunately, was a magnet for such.

With not enough people around to see the real Jane, and/or not realise what would truly help her, her aggressive and disruptive behaviour grew. In time, such characteristics became a part of who she was.

She had small group of friends, which numbered only seven, were the only girls that truly understood her. They were among those who knew what she was really like, whom she could rely on, and vice versa. For Jane, genuine friends did not come along every day. She was used to having herself surrounded by girls, and by the time she was a teenager, she had a dislike for most. If any dared to look at her in a malicious manner or spread any unpleasant rumour about her, similar to how she would deal with anyone thinking of her as an easy target, such girls would soon learn to think twice before repeating such an action.

The exception would be her friends, whom of course, would not be spiteful or bitchy towards her in the first place. If they had an issue with her, they would talk about it. Jane wondered why girls in general were not like them.

There was a strong desire to be studious, but the distraction of boys wanting her attention was too great. It was not real affection, but came close and was more comfortable in the company of the opposite sex.

By the time she was eighteen, and although could have achieved more, Jane had studied enough to pass her exams with above average results. Not excellent, but close enough which suited her just fine.

It was time for her to leave that place behind; move on, though she had not decided where. The way her mind was working, she would rather be homeless than ask for help from anyone.

It was fortunate regarding this, Jane's friends knew what was best for her, more so than herself. They had all found work in a clothes factory, which was far from their long-term goal, but enough to enable them to earn money for a place to live. They had no trouble in talking sense into her, and so with them all living together, it made life easier for the time being and much more enjoyable.

Among many activities they enjoyed, tennis became Jane's favourite. For too long she had been withholding an ever-increasing aggression. The last thing she wanted was to let it loose towards her friends.

It was as if a magician waved his wand and out of nowhere from his hat had found exactly what she needed for so long. Without knowing at the time, there was one more thing she needed; it was not long before she would discover what that was.

Jane would practice at the back of her home, hitting the ball against the wall. To begin with, she loved whacking the ball as hard as she could, but gradually learned control.

It seemed strange at first learning the ins and outs of the rules and conduct. One aspect in particular was the whole points system during a match... *Why is it when a player fails to win a point do they call it* love? *What was the point in 15, and then 30, followed by deuce, and so forth? Why not a simple 1, 2, or... well, whatever another word for deuce could be?* she mused. It seemed as if someone was attempting to be fancy solely for the sake of it.

In time, such ridiculousness within the game became normal.

With a burning desire to play and improve raging through her, she practiced more and more. She would play with her friends on the weekends when they were in the mood; if she could persuade them or at least one of them, she would play during the week.

There had also been debates at the sports centre regarding whether professional female players had the right to the same pay as their male counterparts. It seemed pretty damn clear to Jane... *Simply, no.* Not that she thought female players were not as good as the males, albeit this was often the case. Nor because it was more entertaining watching the men. It was for her, though she imagined many men would rather watch the women play. She knew in an instant that she would gain male attention whenever she stepped onto the court. It was simple, and so damn obvious it was irritating... *The males play for longer!* It would scream inside her head so loud she could not, or more accurate, *I will not hide my irritation* when people failed to see such a blatantly obvious element to the argument; happily relieved to find that her friends thought the same, though not as passionate... *Females play three sets. Males play five. Now shut up and go away!* This is what she would want to say, but instead she would provide a look telling the other person how stupid she thought they were, shake her head, and turn away, thus ending the conversation... *No damn point in wasting good tennis time hearing any more nonsense!* She then would pace towards the nearest wall and whack the ball against it as hard as she could.

There was a man at the sports centre whose job was to coach, if anyone so wished. Since Jane wanted to hone her skills, enter competitions, and practice with someone much more talented than herself, she approached him.

Jim was a tall and slim man, with dark blue eyes who had just turned forty. He had a full head of dark hair, which was in its early stages of greying around the sides. He looked a good ten years younger, in spite of a few of hairs turning grey.

Happy to help coach someone he could tell was enthusiastic about playing and improving her skills. Most important, she was a girl in need of direction. He could tell that he may need to aid her in her journey in such direction a little more firmly than usual; a method he began using over twenty years ago. He felt that with some of the girls, especially Jane, there was a need of its return.

They would practice together as often as Jane had time to spare. In only a matter of months, they became not only good friends, but grew in relationship similar to one on a paternal level. It was kind of so, but not. Jane had found a long sought after male role model. Even though his wife was a motherly figure to her, and she was very good friends with Jim and his wife's two daughters like sisters, concerning Jim, he was, but was not a father figure.

He came close, but... *I dunno. Not that I don't respect him as such. I do. If he scolds me, I accept it; even appreciate it, oddly enough. He's more a strong male figure in my life. Is that not the same thing? I've never had either, really. So... oh, what do I know.*

If Jane needed to seek advice for one thing or another, she would talk with him. If she wanted to get something off her chest, Jim was happy to listen. He genuinely cared about her and wanted what was best for her. To him, he cared about her as if she was his daughter.

She's a girl any man would be proud to call daughter, he thought. *As it stands, she is a member of the family, but I'd rather be considered as a disciplinarian to her. She will soon see more of that side to me. She reminds me, in spirit and attitude, like a young version of my wife,* he laughed to himself. *And how she was in need of several spankings.*

There were occasions when Jane had taken out her frustrations on him; other times, she would surface an attitude. Jim would not hesitate to scold her or threaten to punish her by not playing tennis; the later worked wonders. It only needed implementing a couple of times. The mere threat alone had Jane apologising fast for her behaviour and pleading for him to change his mind.

Jane had yearned for so long a strong male figure in her life that she was close to and respected. Thankfully, she had met Jim. His strength of character, wisdom, and firm but fair manner was what she wanted. She hoped one day to find a boyfriend around the same age as she, or a little older perhaps, with such qualities.

With such a male figure in her life, and a novelty in itself, she often pushed Jim as far as she could to see where he would draw the line. Whenever he had done so, she felt a sense of security; she could misbehave, and no matter what, after a good telling off, he still deeply cared about her. It made her relax; able to be more like herself.

One morning when Jane had stopped by Jim's home to meet him before going to their local training centre, as was the norm, she could not hold herself back from teasing him.

"So... If we ever play mixed doubles, be funny wouldn't it. Jim and Jane, it's kinda like Jack and Jill. Well, not as a couple, couple, you know, not that Jack and Jill were, that I can remember, or care. I mean, after all, you're old enough to be my father. Not that I'd want that, not saying it'd be a bad thing... not to say you're looking older, I mean, well, you could be, being more than ten times my age. Okay, like, almost twice. Your hair, it's going grey. Is it through stress of teaching young girls how to play or is it one of those unfortunate things that can happen in people? You know, premature greying. I see you are going more grey as we speak. That vein in your forehead, was it always there?"

"Stop! Stop right now, young lady. It has been a while since I have spanked a girl your age. You are seriously coming close." Jim knew it was only a matter of time before this situation transpired.

"You wouldn't dare?" Him scolding her for crossing the line was expected and appreciated, but a spanking? She would be lying to herself if she denied curiosity.

"Come here and we will see." Jim sat down on his living room sofa and pointed to his lap.

"I'll stay here, thank you very much," Jane said, wondering whether Jim was serious or not. He looked serious enough. "Besides, you can't do that to me."

"Around twenty years ago, young lady, when I coached down south there were plenty of times I did this and it would not even have raised an eyebrow."

"Well, this isn't a state down south, it's New Jersey. It's also not twenty years ago, if you haven't noticed... or even two hundred years ago, or whenever it was you spanked those girls. You could easily be lying about your age." She pointed at him, looking weary. "Either way, you do realise it's the Ninety's, I mean, Noughty's, or whatever they're calling this decade of ours." Jane paused for a second as her mind wandered, forgetting the imminent danger to her bottom. *I wonder if he knows what decade we're in, let alone the name...*

In that moment, Jim stood and moved a couple of steps towards Jane, taking hold of her wrist and pulling her towards him, noticing but ignoring the startled look upon her face, he lifted her as he sat, and put her across his knee. "Naughty is appropriate considering the amount of girls in need of a spanking these days, yourself included. True, it's clichéd, but this is something that should have been done a long time ago. Do you have anything to say for yourself?"

"Well, yes, as a matter of fact I do. This ain't such a long lost time, a long time ago, like when you were y-ow! Ow! Ow! Ow! Ow!"

Jim prevented Jane from speaking further with a few hard smacks to her skirted bottom. "It is clear that you are not learning, young lady. I think there is a strong need for some firm discipline in your life." He pulled back her skirt and tugged down her panties.

"Hey!" Jane's right arm stretched backwards to cover her bottom, but Jim took her hand and threw it down. Curious as she was about actually going through with a spanking, she thought, *He could at least ask to bare my bottom!*

"It's no good putting your arm back; it will only prolong your spanking. At least I have your attention."

"Yes, you do. What kind of pervert are you-Ouch! Ow! Ow! Will you-Ow!" Through gritted teeth, as Jim kept on spanking, Jane raised her voice, "Will you let me-Ee! Finish a God damn-Ow! Senten-Ah!" She took a deep breath and shouted, "Sentence!"

Jim continued spanking, not prepared to stop or slow down until Jane was more respectful. "I will allow you to speak, young lady, when you know how to speak to me properly, and that means with respect. Now is not the time to sass me while you are across my knee."

As much as she wanted to rebel, Jane knew it would not help improve her current predicament. "Okay, okay, you win-Ow! Ow! Yes-Ow! Ow! Yes, sir."

He spanked her half a dozen more times and then stopped. "Are you ready to speak to me properly?"

"I just said yes, didn... I mean, yes, yes. Yes, sir. Yes." Jane screwed up her face, expecting another barrage of spankings.

"Right, I know you were being more a playful brat. Nevertheless, sometimes you tend to push me as far as you possibly can. Cute as at times it may be, there are other times you have crossed a line. From now on, I will let you know when you are pushing your luck. So take this as a warning, my girl. I will not hesitate to put you across my knee in future. Am I making myself clear, little one?" Jim was confident that he was, so much so, he did not need an answer right away. He pulled up her panties and allowed her to get up off his knee.

Jane became lost in her own world as she stood, biting around the edge of the nails on her left hand; her other hand rubbed her bottom.

He took me across his knee. He has just put me across his knee! *No one had ever done that. Is there a better word for shocked? Anyway, he called me* little one... *I am* not *little! I am of average height. Dammit, I should have said that. Must save it for later.*

Hmm, let me see... spanking, spankings, spank, spanked, smacked and whacked. On the other hand -haha, I like that pun- there is whacking, hiding, walloping, tanning and warming... whoa! Who would have thought there'd be so many words and ways, and more, to describe one thing? The one damn thing that's missing in my life! Well, not anymore, or it would appear. I need to think about this more.

Three things... well, to start: Tennis is a passion... tick number one off the list; I have found the family unit I've always dreamt, with my girlie friends and with Jim's family... tick number two off the list; A strong and kind male figure in my life is Jim... for now, tick number three off the list. I'll always want him in my life, but regarding this, this whole spanking *thing, I would like to find a boyfriend my age or a little older that has a similar strict nature. Oh, that would be just perfect.*

Jim does have a very old-fashioned mindset regarding discipline. Not entirely happy with it, but I am a hundred percent happy with him spanking me -hehe-

It is fascinating... this spanking *thing. I wonder how many girls he has spanked. Be cool to hear about that. Or anyone's experience for that matter. Jim's strict side alone makes me feel I don't need to prove myself as the female equivalent of the Alpha Male. Maybe I can gradually become the girl I want to be. As it turns out, that girl is a little brat -haha- Granted, a playful one, but a brat nonetheless. If I go too far with it then fair enough, I should be spanked.*

Oh, this really is perfect for me. If my old aggressive side arises from time to time, a good spanking will help keep me in check. Much more than tennis ever could. Tennis still rules though... ah, tennis. Need to play...

As a few minutes passed, Jim was wondering what she was thinking. He looked at her as lost in her own thoughts, and thought, *Time to snap her out of that.* "I said, young lady, am I..."

"Oh... yes. Yes, sir. Sorry, sir. Was miles away. You are making yourself clear... for a jackass." Jane gave a cute giggle, waiting for his response.

"What!?" Turning bright red with anger, Jim stood. He was about to say something, but was interrupted.

"Is your face supposed to be that colour? Can't be health... whoa!" Jane found herself unable to finish her cheeky sentence, moving once more as Jim took a swift hold of her arm. Once again, she found herself lifted and placed across his knee. "Did I give you permission to do that?-Ow! Hey, you can't just spank any girl you feel like. I do have rights you know-Ow! Ow! Ow! Ow!" She was happy to be spanked, but would still give Jim a lot of back-chat unless she felt she had way overstepped the line... or was spanked into a whimpering silence or sorriness.

"You have the right to remain silent." Jim pulled back Jane's skirt and continued a much-needed spanking to this little brat, only pausing to speak and to allow her to apologise. "Unless you are ready to say sorry."

"You do realise how lame that was. You're only a tennis instructor. Not a cop." Jane began to snigger, abruptly put to a halt when Jim's hand soundly smacked across her white pantied covered bottom.

He spanked mostly around the outside of Jane's panties. He had done this deliberately. She thought her panties had saved a good part of her bottom. It would soon be a shock to her system, new to this form of discipline, when Jim had such form of protection swiftly removed.

Jane had thought that this time he would only spank her on her panties. It would not take long for her to learn that all spankings would be, at some stage sooner or not much later, on a bare bottom.

Jim carefully spanked around her panties and upper legs, only rarely spanking her panties-covered bottom.

"Ow! Ow! Ow! I'm sorry for giving you attitude, sir-Ow!"

He decided it best to continue spanking as he spoke, smacking carefully around her panties. "I should hope so, my girl. You should learn to think before you speak."

"Ooh! Ooh! Ow! Yes, yes. I will, sir-Ow!"

The area of Jane's bottom, not covered by her panties, increasingly began to shine from a pink to a bright red. The pain increased and made her right arm reach back to protect her stinging bottom.

With a firm voice, he warned, "You have ten seconds to remove your hand, or I will remove your shoe and place that across your bottom. I prefer to use my hand, but be known, you have been warned."

Jane was unsure of what to do. She wanted to keep her hand where it was, but at the same time did not want to imagine the pain of being slippered. The count was fast approaching ten.

"Six... seven... eight... nine..." Jane removed her arm away from her bottom at the last second. "Good girl. Now it's time to lose these." Jim plucked her panties.

Jane gasped as he pulled down her panties to around her knees. It revealed a bare bottom with an area of almost pale white in the shape of where her panties once had been, surrounded the results of her spanking thus far. It was an open target and Jim did not intend to allow it to remain its original colour. He laid his hand to rest on her bottom and could feel how cool this area was in comparison to the spanked, reddened part.

Jane was not going to give any backchat, she decided. Her bottom stung enough without making things worse and reminding Jim of his previous threat to slipper her.

"Right, young lady. Time to match this area with the rest." Jim patted her bottom and then began to spank the pale area.

Jane wriggled with discomfort, using all her willpower to hold herself back from covering her bottom.

Smack after smack after smack, the pale area soon changed from a pale white to a pink, eventually leading to a satisfactory red, matching the other spanked area of her bottom and upper thighs.

As Jim's large hand spanked her now delicate flesh an even brighter red, she cried out each time even louder, turning into a whimper. She decided to let go off all her emotions and let it flow. With that decision, and to her surprise, she felt a sense of relief as tears began streaming from her eyes.

Jane sniffed as Jim paused. "I am sorry, sir."

"Good girl. I believe you have learned your lesson." Jim pulled up her panties and lifted her from his knee. He led her around to his left side and sat her down. Leaning Jane into him, he gave her a cuddle.

Her tears flowed for several minutes. She hugged into him whilst rubbing her sore bottom. All the emotions she wanted to release were able to flow to the surface with those tears.

Jim caressed her hair. "You have been a very brave girl. I do believe that the spankings I have just given were very much over due."

"Yes, sir," Jane agreed. She continued crying, but only

mildly. About five minutes later, she calmed down; there were thoughts she wanted to let out. It was a question she was desperate to have answered, but highly nervous about asking. Her stomach felt as if it was in a knot. "Did you... um, have you... Never mind." She looked down and pretended she had not spoken and continued to hug Jim.

"What is it, little one?"

"Well, er... no, really, it's nothing." She blushed, wishing she had not said a word.

"Listen." Jim rubbed Jane's back. "If you ever feel a need to say anything. As always, do not hesitate to ask."

Jane had taken a deep breath and asked, "Your two daughter's... have you ever spanked them?" She felt embarrassed to ask, but was now counting the seconds, nervously, until it was answered.

"You certainly are a curious thing. The straight answer to that one is no, I haven't."

Jane raised her eyebrows astonished. She knew both his daughters well. They were the same age as her. She could easily imagine both of them over his knee. A wave of disappointment washed over her. "Oh... then tell me this. Why do you feel I am in need of spankings?"

"Because you are in need of spankings," he answered, truthfully.

"You're avoiding the question." Jane found herself somewhat annoyed at his evasiveness, and it showed in her tone. In response to her tone, Jim whacked the side of her thigh. "Ow! Sorry, sir."

"I am glad to hear it. As I was about to say. It was not my desired decision. My wife strongly opposed it. I love my wife deeply. I have only been tempted a few short times. Whenever those times arose, she would discipline them. And it would be without spanking. I am of an old-fashioned mind and feel that girls sometimes need a firm hand placed across their bottoms. But it has only been applied while I've coached. Less so nowadays. In fact, very much less so. However, regarding my daughters, my wife is correct, as she so often is. Just don't tell her I said that."

Amused, Jane giggled. "Of course. I won't."

"Besides, if you would rather I not spank you... let me know. I have to keep reminding myself what time and place I live in."

"I will, sir. As much as I may not want a spanking, I'm sure there will be times in future where they'll be needed."

You certainly have that right, Jim thought, a little amused. "Very well. Then that is what I will do."

"But, and I know it may not be my place to ask. But I would prefer if no one else knew about it." Jane hoped he would agree.

"Yes. That will not be a problem. In today's world, it would not look good. Years ago, and especially when I worked down south, it was acceptable. In certain areas, even today, it still would be. Do not worry. I won't say anything."

Jane wanted to probe further. "Do you spank your wife?"

Surprised by this question, Jim realised it was only a matter of time before it was asked. "That is something between my wife and me."

"That means a *yes*."

"It means, young lady, keep asking and you'll be back across my knee, and I will make use of those rubber shoes you wear for tennis." Jim spoke firmly.

Jane gulped. She knew that was a question too far, but was worth a try. "Yes, sir. What... What about when you worked down south? Surely you can tell me about that, can't you?" She leaned back against the sofa and then sat herself comfortably cross-legged expecting a story. She wriggled into a comfortable position. She had never sat with a spanked bottom before. Uncomfortable as it was, she was enjoying this new experience, knowing that it would not be the case for every spanking in future, depending on how badly she behaved. *It was like a double punishment in a way... having my bottom spanked, and then sitting with a spanked bottom,* she thought.

"I suppose... I suppose, yes. I can tell you about that, if it's of any interest. I can talk about several spankings. Which one, though. Ah... yes, interesting. One was actually to a girl who..." Jim paused, looking across at Jane, "yes. The resemblance between you two in attitude is uncanny.

"It was twenty years ago. Interestingly enough, this was the first time I had spanked. With your current behaviour and need of several reminders to behave, it most certainly won't be the last.

"Interestingly enough, she did look an awful lot like you, and just like yourself, had a burning desire to improve, win matches and enter local competitions. In time, she would move on and succeed in precisely that. But it did not come without hard work... and yes, young lady, several well-earned spankings.

"I can appreciate how old-fashioned this may sound, but it worked. It worked because I would not tolerate attitude from her. And even though she respected me, she would sometimes still push me as hard as she could.

"Bad language on court; smoking; and it goes without saying that laziness in practice would certainly earn a severe bottom warming." Jim leaned back and continued, "The first time I spanked this girl, hmm... she was around your age. She played much better than you did, which should not be a surprise, after all, she had been playing for many years... Hannah was her name.

"Frustrated with her performance at times, she would throw such a temper tantrum, I swear, you would not have guessed her actual age; throwing down her racket, kicking the net, her bag and almost anything else that was in reach.

"After a few times of this, I decided to take a firm control of the situation. To this day, I still don't know why I waited so long before taking her in hand, but I soon made up for that.

"Hannah had behaved so badly on this day, a part of me that wished I were training a whole class; I would have spanked her in front of the lot of them. As it happens, it was only us two training that morning.

"Anyway, as I said, we were practicing one morning, just the two of us. Hannah was experiencing a rare bad day with her performance. She was late, you see, having overslept. To be expected, I was not best pleased.

"I took her aside and calmly said, 'What's the problem? You are not usually late, and if you are... well, you more than make up for it in practice.'

"'Look, I'm just a little tired. Didn't sleep as long as I wanted. To be honest I'm not really in the mood to practice, so back off!'

"'Hey! Don't you dare speak to me like that, young lady. I strongly suggest you change your attitude before you wind up over my knee,' I scolded.

"'Wind up over your knee? Oh, get over yourself. You're not that much older than me. I don't think so. I don't even have to be here. You attempt to, and I'll aim one of these balls directly at yours!' She turned and began to walk away.

"'That's it, you!' I walked and caught her up, took hold of her ear, and began dragging her to the locker-room.

"'Hey you, get off me!' Hannah could not struggle because it pulled even more on her ear. All she could do was walk, powerless to do anything else, and more so when I threatened to tell her parents about her behaviour. 'Nooo! No, please don't that. I'll walk with you, I won't struggle.' She spoke fast, eager for me not to tell them. She told me they were going to fund her part of a vacation that her and her friends had planned as a reward to their daughter for training so hard and doing well with her studies. I imagined that that would not happen if I told them of her behaviour. I gave her the benefit of the doubt, though it did not change my mind. I was still going to spank her.

"Hannah had a very worried look on her face. She was terrified of being taken across my knee. Her face revealed just that. She wanted to run off, but knew I would catch her, spank her, and then I would inform her parents.

"I could see her trembling. She clearly, and rightly so, was not looking forward to it. I can serve hard and fast; she certainly didn't want me to serve my hand across her bottom, but had no say in the matter.

"I led her to my office and let go of her ear. While I moved some of my paper work into a drawer, I told her to stand still. According to my knowledge, Hannah never bit her nails; however, she was this time. 'Stop that, right now, my girl.' I held out her hand and gave it a smack.

"I sat on the edge of my desk and beckoned her towards my lap. She walked slowly until her body was touching my right thigh. I lifted her by her waist and placed her across my knee.

"There were several more spankings I would give her, but of course at that time, I did not know that. 'I do hope this will be the first and very last spanking I need to give you, young lady.' I whacked her skirted bottom several times before Hannah was able to respond.

"In a tone feeling very sorry for herself, she managed to say, 'Yes. Yes, sir. I hope it is-Ow! I mean-Ow! Ow! Ow!

Ow! I will make-Ah! Sure it-Ow! Is, sir!'

"'I most certainly hope so. But I am far from finished with you.' I pulled back her skirt to reveal the traditional white panties. She had a derrière that I will admit, looked very beautiful. I had not yet bared her bottom, but could already tell how she would, no doubt, use it effectively to gain attention from the boys and manipulate them. It would not work on me. She was two years younger than me, but with how she had behaved that morning, you would not have known. Even so, she was a highly attractive girl; more attractive than any girl I've ever met. Nevertheless, her behaviour was so deplorable; her looks would not save her from a much needed bottom warming.

"'Right, little miss,' I scolded, spanking hard and fast. 'I will not be tolerating such attitude. This, I want to make very clear it won't be shrugged off again.'

"Hannah gripped the edge of the desk; her legs kicked up and down as the heat and sting increased and spread across her bottom. 'Ooh! Ah! Ooh! Ooh! Ah! Ah! Ow! Ah! Owie! Owie! Yes-Oww! Oww! Ow! Ow! Ow-Sir'

"I peeled down her panties making Hannah's head snap back in terror. I suppose she was resigned to the fact that she'd be spanked, but was horrified at the thought of me seeing her bare bottom, or worse, a little more. I only had eyes on her bottom, and the task at hand... erm, excuse the pun."

Jane giggled, finding this spanking thing highly fascinating and a touch amusing whenever an apt pun would surface itself.

"Anyway..." Jim coughed, and after clearing his throat, he continued, "At this stage I noticed her face blush a bright red, much more so than her bottom. Her head looked forward again, wanting to avoid looking at me.

"Without hesitation, I had a plan for Hannah's bottom to

match the colour of her flushed face. I kept up with my previous hard and fast pace causing Hannah to kick her legs up and down as she cried out. Her hands lay outstretched gripping the edge of the desk.

"'You better give me one good reason why I should not contact your parents and tell them about your behaviour?'

"A combination of pain and a renewed fear of not travelling with her friends, something she was looking forward to, she shrieked out, 'Ahhh! Nooo! Please no!' Breathless, Hannah had burst into tears; later to discover it was from both these. 'I swear-Ow! Owie, Owie, Owie! I'll behave-Owww! Spank me-Ow! As often as-Ow! You-Ow! Need-Ow! But-Oww! Please, Ow! Ow! Ow! Don't tell-Ow! Them! Ow! Ow! Ow!'

"'That is a very good idea, little one. I won't tell them. But realise, my girl, every time you act up, I'll take down your panties and severely heat you're bare bottom! Do I make myself clear?!'

"'Ow! Ow! Ow! Yes-Ow! Ow! Yes, y-Ow! Yes-Ow! Yes, sir... Ow! Ow! Owie! Owie! Owie!'

"'Good girl.' I stopped spanking and left Hannah to cry across my knee for a few minutes. Her legs had ceased to kick and dangle towards the floor. Her bottom was a bright red, and much more than your recently spanked bottom.

"She thanked me for spanking her and not telling her parents. In time, as I said, I gave her many more, and like with you, it aided in her performance. But for now, with regards to coaching, you are the one that is likely to have her bottom bared and spanked several times to come. We shall see."

Jane was surprised at how shocked she could be in one day. *Wait a second*, she thought. "Isn't your wife's name *Hannah*?"

"Yes, what of it?" Jim knew her next question.

With an exaggerated hand gesture and vocals to match, she asked, "Well, isn't she two years younger than you?"

"Again, you are correct, little one." Jim could have kicked himself for telling her this, but he just got carried away thinking of his wife, enjoying retelling the story of what would soon become the start of their lives together. He would never have told anyone that, it was only because he had just given a spanking that it made him do such a silly thing. "However, It's purely coincidental," he lied.

"Well, what would happen if I *accidentally* asked her?" Jane asked, suspiciously. She was certain that Jim would spank her. *Fair enough,* she thought. *And I will have my answer, which I already know... Haha!*

"I seriously don't think you are going to ask my wife if I spank her. In any case, you do that and I will tell my daughters that I have spanked you. Who know whom they may tell?" He grinned and thought, *Although not tennis, but checkmate.*

Open mouthed, she paused before speaking. She wanted to swear, but she did not want another spanking; well, she did, but not so soon after just receiving one. Grumbling, she admitted, "Fine!" She was happy to know the answer to her previous question, in spite of Jim not actually admitting it was his wife. *He had done so anyway... not in so many words, but still. I'll take it out on him when we play in about fifteen minutes,* she thought.

"Come on. Time to play." He stood and walked over to pick up his bag near the main TV in the living room.

Jane gave him a highly brat-filled look before she had no choice but to smile as she stood.

I will kick your fat ass on court for not getting my own way, she thought, or so she thought.

"What was that?" Jim asked; as to be expected, not too pleased.

Jane could have sworn she thought what she had just said. *Unless, hmm... he had psychic powers.* She looked at him suspiciously before gulping. Panicked, she rushed out a sentence, "Um, Um, I said, sir: I will show my class on court, now let's get on our way!" She raised her eyebrow, quite proud of her quick thinking, hoping it would be enough to fool him.

Not fooled for one moment, Jim smacked her bottom hard, ordering sharply, "Get out that door and into my car... and now, young lady!"

Jane wasted no time in doing as she was told.

As soon as she was out of earshot, Jim chuckled... *Why did that just almost sound like a bad line from a classic* Billy Ocean *song.*

After their training session, Jane was more than happy to head to the locker room and have a cold shower. Her performance was breathtaking, being very true to her actual words that earned her a smacked bottom just before they left the house.

The shower eased the sting from her bottom; surprisingly, it still lingered. Her bottom would get used to it, she hoped. She wondered if too many spankings would ruin the appearance of her bottom.

Hmm... But then again, Hannah still has a well-shaped bottom. After all, she must have had many spankings over the years, not to mention the ones she must still receive.

If I keep myself in shape, the same should apply to my own. It must... it will... so, there!

Jane glanced back to catch a glimpse and rubbed it every minute or so as she washed. Leaving the shower and drying herself, she turned her back, looked over her shoulder and into the mirror, and perched out her bottom. She enjoyed viewing the reflection of her well-shaped and well-spanked bottom, so much so, that she found it an effort to take away her eyes from such a sight.

I hope to earn many more of these spankings in future. It feels so right to look in the mirror and see the sight of my reddened cheeks.

Year after year, Jane continued training hard. Equally, if not harder, according to her bottom, were the spankings, which accompanied this and came to be a regular part of her life. There were, of course, times when she would struggle and resist; however, she knew it was necessary.

Before any competition match, at Jane's request, Jim took her across his knee. With a hard spanking, she felt a relief that enabled her to focus on the game and play at a level that became near impossible to defeat. If anyone asked her for her secret, she would reply, "Dedication and hard work." Although true, a well-placed hand across her bottom was likewise important; she would never tell anyone that part.

Prior to a local tournament, Jim needed to leave town to attend to family matters. He made it back in time for Jane's match, but her performance was not at its usual level. If it continued, she would most certainly lose.

She was in need of a firm word at the interval.

Rubbing his eyes in frustration, Jim was trying to figure out Jane's lack of usual quality performance. "I have no idea what's happening out there. It's nowhere near what you're capable of achieving."

Equally frustrated, but for different reasons, her posture slumped; her elbows on her thighs and hands in her face. "Perhaps it's the lack of heat."

"Excuse me?" Frustrated and now confused, he tried to

remain calm. "It's a nice day out there. Speak to me properly. I know I had to go away for a week. Granted, it was unfortunately timed, but you were performing excellently in practice. I've never seen you play like this. Oh yes, before you need to get back out there do tell me about this... heat."

She sat up, and told him plainly, "You know what. Spanking. I've been craving one all week. I can't think straight. I can't just ask any stranger on the street to give me one. And it's one I'm in need of before a match. You're my coach, you should of known that I would need it."

"Ah, of course. You are right. I should have, and by the way, it's *should have*, not *should of*."

"You're kidding me, right?" Jane could barely believe what she was hearing. "I'm having the worst game of my life and all you can think of is my grammar?"

Jim was about to say something, but decided against it. In its place, he said, "Again, you're right. I can be the worst culprit." He suddenly thought of a different tactic that might result in Jane's performance bouncing back to its normal high standard. "If you lose this match, my girl," he spoke more firmly, pointing his finger towards her.

"Isn't it rude to point?" Jane enjoyed Jim's firm voice, even a little amused. She was unable to withhold her cheekiness, no matter how accurate.

"Yes..." He looked up to the sky, wanting more than ever to smack this girl's backside, one arm behind his back and crossing his fingers, he continued, "If you lose this match, my girl, I will never spank your bottom again."

Jane's mouth dropped. "What?!"

"You heard me, my girl."

"No!" Sounding very much like a little brat with a look of dissatisfaction at such a statement, Jane stood; with purpose, but making sure not too hard, she kicked Jim in the shin.

Yelling out and hopping, rubbing his shin, he yelled, "You f..." He sucked his teeth in an attempt to hold back from swearing. "You little brat!" He took a firm grip of her arm, turned her around and gave a hard whack across her bottom.

"Ow! I thought you sai..." Unable to finish what she was about to say, Jim sat on the edge of locker-room bench and threw her across his knee.

Jim pulled pack Jane's skirt and sharply pulled down her panties followed by several solid smacks across her bare bottom. "You ever," he scolded, his hand causing her well-deserving cheeks to wobble with each and every thwack; a loud echo filling the locker-room, which fortunately for Jane, no one outside could hear. "And I mean, ever do that again, I will spank you where everybody, including the local press, can see. Do I make myself clear?!"

"Ow! Ow! Ah! Ouch! Ow! Ow!" Jane managed to catch her breath for a moment, and answer, "Yes, you do, sir."

Jim pulled up her panties and let her stand. "While we have a few minutes left, young lady, you will sit your bottom down and listen."

As he stood, about to walk, he forgot the impact of Jane kicking him; his newly formed limp had caught him off guard. As such, he came very close to falling over.

Highly amused, but fighting to suppress a giggle, Jane covered her mouth as she snickered. Seeing the not so amused look on Jim's face, she quickly sat down and shot a look to the left and right, as a part of her attempts to look innocent.

"Don't you even dare, my girl!" Jim scolded. "If it wasn't for the fact that you have a match right now, I would have given you such a hiding. In fact, I don't know why I am not doing so. You deserve to go out and have the possibility of everyone seeing you with a well spanked backside."

Jane was doing her best not to brat him by saying, *I don't care*; of course in reality, she did. Jim was in the mood where he was likely to follow up any threat... *Well, minus the part about not spanking me.* She had proven that if provoked, he most certainly would. It was clear, either win or lose, albeit knowing it was a win to come, she was in big trouble and in for a very heavy spanking.

With that realisation, there was no need for a pep talk. Jim knew this as he noticed how perkier Jane had become. He clapped his hands. "Right, stand up. We have a game to win. First things first, bend over. I need to see if your bottom is reddened or has any sign of a hand print."

Jane did as she was told. "I'm sure my butt looks fine," she said, more hoping that knowing.

Jim raised Jane's skirt and pulled down her panties a little, but enough to bare most of her bottom. "Everything seems to look normal." Normal as in a little redness was visible. It would fade fast soon enough. Her panties would cover the slightly reddened part of her bottom.

He held her in place with his left hand. Jane knew what was to follow; her face winced in anticipation.

As she suspected, Jim's other hand sharply landed across her bottom; landing two heavy smacks across each cheek, one at a time. "I will deal with you later, young lady. Now get out there and win!" he said firmly.

"Yes, sir!" Jane pulled up her panties. With a smile, she picked up her racket and ran out onto the court with a spring in her step. It was time, she determined, to give her opponent a damn good spanking, so to speak.

A Soldier Returns
(A pre/post World War Two spanking story)
~Brat No. 6: Sarah~

Waking up early became something of a habit in wartime; the same applied otherwise. For now, and after so long, it was time to grow accustomed to the latter.

After so long, it was finally over. A 1945 without war... well, there will always be wars, sadly, I'd imagine. But not for me. Not anymore.

Old habits are still the worst to break, and so without thinking, Jack threw back the blanket and quickly got to his feet. No sooner had he done so, he gave out a loud sigh of relief, got back into bed, and looked over at his wife, Sarah, still sleeping. He kissed her forehead and lay staring at the ceiling.

Years before, which seemed a lifetime in itself, whenever it was safe to daydream, Jack would be lost in such a moment. Dreams of lying in bed with Sarah. Dreams of lying in bed with Sarah and holding her, both feeling at ease.

At long last, no more dreaming, he thought as he glanced at Sarah. *I love you, my little sweetheart, more than you can possibly imagine.*

The pattern on the ceiling drew his attention once more.

The birds outside were talking and going about their early morning business; the very same birds that woke him were now such a joy to hear. He never gave it a thought before as to what they might be talking about; for now, he found enjoyment in being able to contemplate something so silly and trivial.

I believe it will be a nice day. One more week remained until he returned to work, and the future was looking very bright, including Sarah's cute bottom.

Jack recalled, after the demobbing process, the train ride home; thoughts of nature drifted across his mind. Nature had never interested him in the past; fighting in the fields of Europe had changed that. Those fields were in vast contrast to the deserts of North Africa. Whenever he had time to admire his surroundings, the surroundings untouched by fighting, such appreciation stayed with him.

He also remembered a feeling that at one point began to pour through his entire body. Although the train was packed, that feeling remained. Before the train had filled with people going about what was now their post-war business, he was fortunate to have found a seat available next to the window, where he gazed out onto the fields as it journeyed through the countryside. That feeling... relaxed.

It had been so long since he felt that he could truly do such a thing.

Even though I enjoyed soldiering, I can actually say with relief that the army is behind me... the war, thank God, is now behind me. Ahead of me is my little sweetheart... my little sweetheart. He knew his job at the railway happily awaited his return, which was an additional comforting thought. *Another thing I'll look forward to.*

It was not long before his mind returned to his little sweetheart.

As the train approached closer to home, a combination of excitement and anxiety replaced all calmness at the thought of reuniting with his wife.

They had always written to each other, but he had never had the chance to visit her. After leaving England around the middle of 1940, he had not seen Sarah in years. That time apart was painful and felt doubled. From her last letter, she was very excited at his return. She was proud to be his wife. He loved it when she said that or wrote it. She was, as he had hoped, relieved that he would never be away for so long again. She also warned him never to do that again, the thought alone was simply unbearable. Such a warning amused Jack, but naturally, he knew how she felt.

When they were finally re-untied, he recalled how the nerves in his stomach were working in overdrive. Happy to be home, he hoped she was honest in her letters. If so, it would be a good day.

He knew she loved him.

Would she still, after actually seeing me in person after all these years? Photos are one thing. I should not be so silly. I know she loves me. Doesn't help how I feel. Why would she reject another if she didn't love me? That being so, this is not easy now I am actually so close to her.

Stepping off the train and walking through his town, familiar as ever, felt good. Fortunately, he was pleased to read in Sarah's letter, it had escaped the heavy bombings other towns and cities faced from the Luftwaffe.

His final minute of walking, arriving at his front gate, and then knocking on the door was like nothing he had ever experienced; a feeling he did not want to repeat. After dreaming of this moment for so long, it was now a reality.

Why is breathing steady more difficult in reality? Almost as bad as going into battle. Well, I'm here now. Home.

That final minute of walking had increased when he could not bring himself to open the gate; walking to the end of the street, he took a deep breath, turned around, and made a very slow walk back to his house.

Then, and what seemed slower than usual, the door opened. It had not seemed real, but at last was happening. Jack would later discover, unsurprisingly, that she was feeling the same nerves as he. Every time for the previous few months, Sarah had been dreading and yet wished for a certain knock at the door.

When she saw him for first time in years, staring in disbelief, she found herself double-checking this man from head to toe; lasting only a few seconds to confirm this was no illusion.

With the biggest and brightest smile Sarah had given from before her husband departed for war, not realising how long it would be before they would see each other again, unable to speak, she held out her arms.

With that smile and arms opened wide, all nervous thoughts and worries disappeared. He gave Sarah the biggest hug that he could remember. It was different, more a gratefulness to be back home alive and have the chance to hold her. In return, Sarah squeezed him harder than ever. She refused to release her grip for fear of him going away again.

Holding his wife with one hand, he leaned to the side to pick up his bag, and lifting Sarah from the ground, he walked into their home.

Kicking the door closed and dropping his bag near the side table in the corridor, he gently lowered his wife so her feet were back on the floor, still holding her; he closed his eyes for a moment, inhaled deeply, and then breathed out a huge sigh of relief to be home. He lifted his wife, cradling her; she held him around his neck. He walked slowly into their living room, looking around the home that he had been dreaming of for so long. Everything seemed almost as it was when he left, but that would come later. All he wanted to do was look at his wife. He imagined his appearance was that of someone much older, though he knew she would always disagree if he mentioned it. Sarah, on the other hand, in spite of her own hardships, had not aged at all.

Jack continued his slow walk towards their sofa; he sat down, sitting her on his lap. There, he held his adoring wife for an hour, neither one of them wanting to let go. Sarah spent ten of those minutes with tears of joy and relief.

After about an hour of holding one another, Jack began tenderly caressing Sarah. It was something he had yearned to do for so long. Inevitably, other desires kicked in and soon they kissed passionately.

Barely able to speak, Sarah released the words she had been yearning to say for so long. "Take me, Daddy!"

Without a second thought, he picked her up and took her to their bedroom.

Sarah did not hesitate to place herself across her husbands lap at the first chance and request a spanking that she had craved for years. Jack did not disappoint. That spanking, followed by lovemaking, was something ever so satisfying; that day and night felt heavenly satisfying.

If ever one could imagine such, then imagine five years of a brat craving the husband she deeply loved; craving that he take her in hand and give her a damn good spanking; craving for her man to kiss and caress her.

Then, after a good spanking, still with her bottom burning like the fire within her burning with desire for her man; to cuddle into as he holds her, but not before feeling his manliness hard inside her again and again.

Furthermore, being able to release into energy those feelings of not knowing if she would ever see him again, dreading every knock at the door for fear of the worst; resisting temptation, wanting to remain faithful to her one and only man. Having to put on a brave face like the rest of the country, but not wanting to, wanting her man to deal with issues she considered a man's place; for him to take care of her while in her own way, look after him.

As for such a brat's husband, a man who had many times faced battle and the fear of not returning home; also the unpleasant thought of how distraught she would be if he did not. His desires similarly paralleled hers.

If she wants her bottom smacked so hard, then the room shall be filled with a loud echoing sound of a bare bottom receiving a heavy hand... and the cries of my little girl feeling the sting.

Both were finally able to release into energy all their fears, tension and doubt that each had felt.

Imagining thus far, then imagine the explosive and passionate sex that would follow the spanking; repeatedly, and with so many variations, releasing further tension whilst appropriately expressing their love, so long overdue.

It was for both of them a truly exhausting, yet exhilarating and memorable day and night... a magical taste of heaven on earth.

Almost distracted with thoughts of lovemaking, Jack realised if he had acted like the *Daddy* she wanted, her bad behaviour the following week would not have reached its peak. Then again, if he had, then perhaps neither would have formed such closeness after firmly taking his wife in hand. It may have taken a lot longer to feel the special bond, more so than ever before, they now had between them.

Sarah slept naked that night and mostly, understandably, on her stomach. He pulled back the sheets and viewed his wife's punished bottom. Still very reddened, he caressed it slowly and tapped it a couple of times, then put back the sheets over his wife, and allowed her to sleep.

He laid back, closed his eyes, and thought back to when they first met. Moreover, he thought how her calling him *Daddy* had progressed from one level of humour to a form of affection. From there, still a form of affection, it now included respect for him as a strict disciplinarian. He had not realised at the time, but it was what she wanted all along.

They met during the summer of 1938 at a dance hall. Sarah was seventeen; Jack was twenty-six. It was a calm and warm Saturday evening.

Jack had nearly missed the chance to meet the love of his life.

It was ever so rare for him to be unwell, but this time, although feeling much better, he was in no mood to join his friends that night; only on the persistent urgings of his friends did he succumb. For the most part, he was well enough, having recently recovered from flu. *As if that happens in the summer?* he thought.

He decided he might as well, but was not going to drink. He knew that would change when the first drink passed his lips.

A well-dressed and handsome man, Jack had caught the eye of many a girl. He was tall, dark and owner of a smile that women seemed to enjoy; being a single man, he took pleasure in flirting with them. He loved female company, but had no serious intention of entering a serious relationship. He was not sure what he wanted, but later found all the answers would fall into place with one such lady.

At the bar with his friends, Jack had noticed a group of girls entering the hall. There was seldom a man amongst them. They assumed it was a celebration of sorts, no doubt a birthday. One girl had caught Jack's eye. She was a beautiful little thing, petite and so cute. Her mousy blonde hair and blue eyes had shone something that Jack found irresistible. This unknown, cute girl was wearing a red dress that enhanced her almost indescribable beauty. He hoped she was not with a man. There was a lot of attention focussed on her, but no man was with her. Jack hoped she was as a nice a girl as she was cute. He was determined to find out.

He excused himself from his friends; they toasted with each other when they saw him approach a girl who was centre of attention.

Jack offered to buy her a drink. A handsome man he was and equally generous, providing drinks for those in her group, they all warmed towards him in no time. It was not long before he found the name of this young girl.

Sarah.

He wanted so much to talk with Sarah alone; telling the group that he would keep her safe whilst outside, he then introduced his single friends to the single women among the group. Together, arm in arm, Jack and Sarah walked outside for some fresh air and made their way towards a near by stream.

With no one around, they enjoyed their time together on this beautiful warm night as they talked, holding hands. They walked passed a bench and decided to sit for a moment. Jack liked how it felt when Sarah leaned into him.

Their conversation led in the direction that Sarah was more interested. In her mind, there was blueprint of a man that had she wanted and dreamed of for so long; she was at an age where she was sure of what she wanted and would not settle for anything else.

"You certainly need this night air. Those few drinks have gone to your head remarkably fast," he commented.

"Well, I have a little secret." Sarah remained dignified, albeit a tiny light headed from the drink. "I don't often drink. I'm only seventeen, you see. As of midnight tonight, I turn eighteen. My parents never allowed me to drink. They believe I am with a few friends. This is not untrue. I just never told them where," she giggled, mischievously.

"You are a very naughty girl, aren't you?" He noticed how her naughty giggle had made her even cuter, if that was possible.

"Well, what are you going to do about it?" These words were not from a girl who had drunk too much; her tone had made her case clear. Especially when she had not deviated her glance from him after she spoke these words until he replied.

For the first time, Jack purposely looked away as if distracted by something. Sarah's gaze remained fixed upon him, and so he thought of the only thing that came to mind. Facing her, he replied, "Well, if you were in my charge, I most certainly would have put you over my knee, young lady. It's clear you're in need of a good smacked bottom." He smiled thinking all this was a game.

Sarah let out a little gasp, which he did not know, was hitting the spot. What became very clear was that she was as attracted to him as he was to her.

"After all, since I look older than my years and you, sweetheart, looking youthful, I could easily pass as somebody such." Jack laughed, amusing himself -by the look on Sara's face- if no one else.

Sarah lightly hit him. Speaking firmly for a change, she told him, "You do not." Returning to her usual sweet tone, she added, "But then, if you insist, I will have to call you

Daddy. In fact, I've decided. You are." She giggled happily as she hugged him.

"I believe then... as this *Daddy* to you," Jack said, still thinking it was all a joke was very much serious about what he would say next. "I will have to begin courting you." He liked this girl and wanted to make sure no man had the chance of snatching her away; she had no plans of having anyone other than him snatching her away. Although he was not thoroughly certain of his feelings, he wanted the chance to explore the possibilities.

"I hope you do more than that. Did you just tell me that I was in need of something?" Sarah waited anxiously, wondering with hope. *Would he really do this?*

"Ah, yes. Indeed, I did, young one. Come here." He held her waist and laid her across his lap, and slapped her bottom four times.

"Hmm..." Sarah said flatly, wanting to say... *Mmm, well that's a start.* She instead decided, "That was hardly anything. Is that your best?" she challenged. Jack smacked her bottom once more. "Still didn't hurt," noted Sarah, still not impressed. That was until his hand smacked down upon her little bottom several times a lot harder. "Ow! Ooh! Oww! That's better, Daddy."

Jack found that he was enjoying himself as he rubbed this cheeky girl's little bottom.

"You must know, Daddy, I do have personal beliefs," she said. *I have taken my chance up till this point... successfully, too. I may as well see how far I can take it,* she thought.

Sarah was almost terrified of him thinking she was weird for wanting to have her bottom smacked.

"Beliefs?" Jack found it hard to stop caressing her cute bottom. He suddenly realised there was no reason to, so he continued.

"I firmly believe if a smacked bottom is to be given, then it should be upon a bare bottom. Otherwise, there is no point." She nervously awaited his response.

"I can see the reasoning behind that." Jack had not treated a girl like this before. It was enjoyable, though he could sense, obvious that is was, she wanted a proper hiding. He was certain she would do something to earn him putting her across his lap once more, but her little bratty comments made him want to show her how hard he could smack. *Right here... and yes, now,* he thought.

He slowly pulled back her red dress. She had wonderfully shaped legs and an even more wonderful little bottom.

It became exciting to peel down her white knickers to reveal such a beautiful and cute little bottom in its barest form. It was certainty overdue a few good slaps. "Are you ready to be a good little girl... or do I need to give you a damn good hiding?" He felt his hands wander across her bottom without giving it a thought.

"No, Daddy, I am not!" Sarah replied, childishly.

Jack glanced around to see if anyone was within distance to hear or see. "We'll soon see about that, my girl."

When he was certain no one was around, he unleashed several heavy smacks across her bottom that caused her cutely to cry out. "Ow! Ow! Ow! Ow-Yes! Ooh! Ah! You can smack hard. Yes, Daddy. I'll be a good little girl. I will, I will!" Sarah cried out desperately, and with good reason. A firm hand smacking bare flesh produced a highly pleasant sound to both their ears as it filled the night air. If someone had heard or even seen Jack slapping her bottom, whoever it was might well have ignored it, assuming a husband was disciplining his wife or something similar, but she had no desire for that. Only to know if Jack would, and as she discovered, he did. "I think we should return, sir, before someone comes looking for us."

"You are quite right, my darling." Jack pulled her up and let her stand and sort out her clothing. "You look so cute pulling up your knickers after a smacked bottom." He thought for a moment. "Odd. I've smacked you, but I haven't kissed you. I must correct that at once. Come here, young one." He patted his lap.

"Yes, Daddy." Sarah, after pulling up her knickers and straightening her dress, did as Jack bade her; she happily sat on his knee.

"Well, according to my watch, we are now entering a new day, my darling. Happy birthday, my little sweetheart." Jack stroked her cheek and gave her a kiss. He told her to stand, and when they both had, he held her firmly and leaned her backwards. He followed with a sensual kiss, which made them both tingle with excitement.

Glancing at Sarah, Jack thought of that first year together. It was almost indescribable the happiness her presence had in his life. Without a doubt, he knew there was something very special about this girl.

Sarah enjoyed very much referring to Jack as *Daddy*. None of his previous girlfriends had ever called him this. Even so, he did enjoy this term of affection. She seemed to enjoy him being masterful with her, even more so when he threatened to tan her backside.

Throughout the year, there was the occasion when Jack would smack her bottom, but would only be a single slap or a few in quick successions; only four times during that year had Jack taken Sarah over his knee.

Deep down wanting more, she decided to take her time in moulding him into the strict disciplinarian that she wanted. He had potential. Time would take care of the rest.

In time, Jack would realise this. He would have realised

long before had war not came along in September 1939.

Sarah was proud that her boyfriend had a desire to join up. She thought it would be over by Christmas; on his return, they would marry and begin a happily married life, and in time, start a family.

Jack knew better. Opinions were similar to that of the Great War. It was not over for Christmas.

Events had moved swiftly, but one thing was clear. Jack wanted to go to war with Sarah as his wife.

During one of their many enjoyable walks through the park, he spoke to her about the chances of the war lasting perhaps even two or three years, which would lead to a lengthy and unwelcome separation.

Their conversation would lead onto marriage, as it had several times before. This time was different. He got on one knee and proposed. He did not yet have a ring, but that was of little importance for Sarah, replying *yes* without hesitation. He was in no way nervous about proposing. After all, it was what they both wanted.

Jack was proud to become a soldier, and more importantly, a married man. He knew Sarah was equally proud to be a married woman, in particular one who was wife to a very good-looking soldier. *Well, maybe not the latter,* he thought, laughing to himself.

Thoughts of marriage, joining the army, training, and war drifted across Jack's mind as he caressed his wife's heated bottom.

Choosing to think more of his wife than the army, or the war for that matter, he recalled how beautiful she looked on their wedding day.

Her long white dress truly enhanced her beauty. He felt so blessed. She, too, felt blessed, and took great pride in announcing her vows; for her, the best part of all: to love, honour and obey.

It was, up until then, the best day of their lives.

Sarah had moved in with him on the day of their wedding; since they could not afford the honeymoon they wanted, this became a proxy-honeymoon until after the war. Her parents offered to pay for such, but finally moving in with each other, Jack and Sarah were more than happy to wait until they saved enough money. Prior to this, she had enjoyed planning a touch of re-decoration to his home… *Our home now,* she thought happily. *I'll make a start tomorrow.*

Jack was pleased she wanted to make it just as much her home… *After all, it now was,* he pleasantly thought. *Besides, it's in need of a woman's touch.*

That night, and much to Sarah's delight, she would find herself over his knee after he slowly and sensually undressed her.

"I'm not so sure that you will always obey me, little girl. So this is certainly needed for you to remember, even more so for lying in church."

"But Daddy, I wanted to mean it-Ow! Yes Daddy." Only in her underwear, she sighed happily when Jack peeled down her knickers. Even though she was happy, Sarah's smile soon changed as she felt his hand smack hard across her little bottom. "Ooh! Ooh! Ow! Ow! Ow-Daddy! Ow! Ow!…"

Still caressing his wife's little bottom, Jack had accidentally woken her. She rolled over and smiled at him, still half asleep.

"Come here, my little sweetheart." Jack allowed Sarah to cuddle into him and fall back to sleep. Caressing her smooth back and bottom some more, he thought of his transformation into the strict disciplinarian that Sarah had longed for.

He was so happy to be home and to be with her after such a long war that he had forgotten about her desires for him to be strict. Her letters focussed on her activities and of missing him. With the thought of her letters being censored during wartime, not wanting anyone other than Jack knowing, she chose not to include, he soon would realise, what she was also missing... a soundly smacked bottom from her loving husband.

When he did not become, as she had hoped or expected, the strict husband he had potential to be, and pre-war was steadily becoming, her attitude developed and increased, reflecting her bitter disappointment and resentment.

Jack had noticed changes regarding Sarah's attitude all too frequently. Two weeks was enough. *No more. This attitude will stop, and stop it will, right now!*

It was just before lunch when Jack decided to comment on her behaviour when she began to order him to sort out the back yard in a very disrespectful manner.

"This will to stop, right now, Sarah," he warned her, knowing her reaction. It mattered not. He was going to deal with this situation appropriately.

Furious that her husband was attempting to take control, she screamed out, "Excuse me? *This stops, right now?*" She spoke mockingly of his voice, as if it was weaker than it really was, before returning to her own angered tone, "What stops, right now? Taking control of the household? Being head of the household? You come back expecting me just to let you take control of things. Even as outlandish it seems, obey you? Do not make me laugh... huh! Not a chance."

"Yes, young girl, I will..."

"Don't you, young girl, me," she interrupted.

"I will *young girl* you!" he scolded, raising his voice, speaking more firmly. "Do not even question who the head of this household is. You will obey me, and as such, don't you even dare *think* of speaking to me like that!" Jack took a deep breath, calming himself. "It will come to a stop."

"Oh, shut up, you fool."

"This is a final warning, my girl. I have been far more lenient recently, much more than I should have been. Don't think for one second, young girl, you're too big to be put over my knee!"

"What?! Yeah, I'd like to see you try." Sarah, challenging him furiously, was not prepared to go anywhere willingly with this weak man, let alone over his knee.

Just you try it, if you're man *enough!*

Without a word more to say, Jack stormed out of their living room and headed towards the kitchen.

Not at all happy with what seemed his inability to stand up to her, and frustrated that he even dared. This man before her was not the man she married. Before the war, all he needed to do was to glance at her in a certain way and she knew she had overstepped the line. Nowadays, not only had she overstepped it, she left it miles behind. They had not yet discussed what he went through during the war, but for him to walk away like that, it seriously lowered her opinion of him.

"Yeah, that's right. Shows what you are, doesn't it. Walk away. Run away. How the hell you won the bloody war, I'll never know, you cowardly bastard!"

Storming back into their living room, looking more cross than Sarah had ever seen Jack, her eyes widened as she saw a wooden spoon in his right hand. Without time to run or say anything, he took a firm hold of her arm and was taking her to the dining room.

Taming Of The Brat

Sarah knew she had finally pushed her luck as far as it could go; soon she would pay the price. Before she had time to think of a way of escaping his hold, they both were in the dining room. Jack pulled out a chair from the dining room table, sat, and pulled her down over his knee. Without a word, he altered her position so that her bottom was in perfect aim. He remained silent for a little while longer and allowed the wooden spoon to speak for him as he began to tan his wife's backside.

Thwack followed thwack; the force of the wooden spoon fell heavily upon Sarah's bottom. Her skirt and knickers provided only little protection from the pain. She knew worse was to come when he bared her bottom.

The only sound for what seemed longer than a few minutes was that of Sarah yelping out in pain, paralleled with that of the wooden spoon connecting with her bottom, which filled the room.

"Right, young girl. I hope that has caught your attention." Jack's firm voice, as well as the hard surface of the wooden spoon, had certainly made the appropriate impact on her wayward attitude.

"Yes, I..." Sarah cried out, wanting to apologise and not receive more of a tanning; she was much more in the mood to talk calmly and with greater respect.

Jack whacked her bottom twice rapidly. "You will not interrupt me, my girl."

Doing as he told her by remaining quiet, Sarah was not surprised when Jack raised her skirt and lowered her knickers. After all, she was receiving a *spanking*, as she had heard a few GI's comment on what she needed when she was with her friends during the war. It sounded funny when they said it like that.

Whatever people decided to name it, that's just what I'm getting... and deserve.

Moreover, in her opinion, there was no point in doing so over clothes.

It should be on the bare bottom or not at all. Ooh, I may regret saying that. Nevertheless, considering his mood, he probably would have, anyway.

She was surprised Jack had not put her over his knee when she first surfaced an attitude towards him.

Some of my friends would not have dared speak to their men in such a way. Then again, some men would not dare speak to their wives like that. In part, this would pin point such bad influences.

Such influences, she knew, were not person she was or wanted to be.

All Sarah had wanted was to see signs of her old husband, a man that knew how to take charge. He had seemed too relaxed. She realised he needed something to shake him back to normal, and having to deal with her poor attitude towards him, was just what was needed. She knew well a certain phrase... *be careful what you wish for*; it would certainly apply here.

Jack, so furious with his wife, was not ready to prematurely end a much needed lesson in respect. He whacked the wooden spoon down hard upon Sarah's bare bottom and scolded her every time it heavily made its impact across her ever-increasing, reddening, delicate flesh. "Don't... You... Even... Dare... Speak... To... Me... Like... That... Ever... Again!" He paused only for a moment. "You have no idea what I went through, and to say that..." As Jack spanked Sarah, all she could do was cry out as every thwack painfully warmed her bottom; his fast pace continuing, only pausing when he scolded her.

"I love you so much... and am very proud of you. How you have coped while I was away... Doing your bit as well... How your confidence has grown... and how you still are the same girl I fell in love with... But... this recent... behaviour... can no longer be tolerated..."

Sarah had already begun to cry, very apologetically. She was not only crying because of the spanking, which was extremely painful, but was disappointed in herself for not trying to understand why her husband needed time to relax and slowly pull himself together.

Sarah kicked her legs up and down, knowing it would not ease the pain, but doing so without thinking. Kicking her legs became a little awkward due to her knickers sliding down to around her ankles early on in the spanking.

She started crying out even louder as her bottom turned a cherry red. Whilst her tears flowed, she felt a huge sense of relief from the guilt that had surfaced when she realised how badly she behaved.

"You have been behaving like a little brat... and next time, mark my words, I will tan your backside... just like I am now... There will not be any half a dozen warnings, either... I have leaned that much myself... Do I make myself clear, young girl?"

"Ow! Ow! Ow! Yes-Ow! Ow! Ow! Yes, Daddy," Sarah sobbed. "Please..." She tried to speak, tasting some of the tears that flowed down her face, "I am-Ow! Ah! Ah! Ow! Owie-sorry! Daddy! Ow! Ow! Ow! I'm really, really sorry... Oww! I will-Ow! behave as a-Ah! a w-Ow! Ow! A wife..." She took a deep breath as the wooden spoon relentlessly pounded her bottom, which now felt as if it was on fire; its appearance was also very similar. "Should towards her-Owww! husband."

"I am happy to hear that. But do not think I am through with you, my girl, just yet... Along with changing your attitude, young girl... You will not use that bad... language... again. That is not how a beautiful... young lady talks... You didn't use that language before... and I have no idea why you think I will allow you to start... or continue as you have in my absence..."

"Yes-Ow! Ow! Ow! Yes-Ow!" she cried out, hysterically. "Yes, yes, yes-Owww! Yes, Daddy... I promise, I promise!" Her desperation was ever increasing, wanting to let her Daddy know of her agreeing one hundred percent with him.

He is in the right, she thought. She knew that she deserved every singe thwack of that awful wooden spoon.

"Good girl." Jack paused, thoughtfully looking down upon his wife; it felt so normal having her in such a position.

Laying limp over Jack's knee and with a well-spanked bottom, Sarah hoped it was over. She reached back and tried to rub her bottom. Not stopping his wife from giving some small relief, he decided to take her hand and rest it on her back.

Thinking the spanking was about to continue, Sarah cried out once more in desperation, "No, please!"

"Shhhh." Jack said, soothingly. He let go of his wife's hand, and stroked her hair. "I am not going to continue."

Jack began to rub Sarah's poor little bottom. *Very, very warm*, he thought. He felt better for spanking his wife. She both deserved and needed it... *Undoubtedly*. He allowed her to get up off his lap; holding her hand, he led her upstairs.

"I believe a certain young girl will need an early night tonight," Jack commented as he entered their bedroom.

"Yes, Daddy," replied Sarah, still sobbing away with her head lowered, moved a lot easier since her knickers became loose from her ankles and left on the stairs.

Removing her skirt, Jack sat on their bed and leaned up against the headboard. Beckoning Sarah to sit on her side of the bed, the right, next to him, he leaned her into him and gave her a good cuddle, and allowed her to cry some more whilst he rubbed her little bottom.

"I only misbehaved because I wanted the old you back." Sarah's tone sounded more childish than she meant.

"It's all right, sweetheart. Though next time you want to discuss anything with me, come to me. Even if it means I am cross with you. I don't ever want us at a stage where we can no longer talk to each other," he said in a very soft manner. "I needed time to get used to feeling at ease. I was enjoying it. Just because I am, it doesn't mean I won't be strict with you when needed. I know it took a little time, but you can guarantee... it will not take so long from now on."

Glad to hear those words and still sobbing, Sarah smiled. "Yes, Daddy, I am happy with that."

For several minutes more, they held each other in silence. There was calmness in the air; the spanking had created such an atmosphere, bringing relief to them both.

"Jack... Daddy, will I be receiving any more spankings if I am naughty or disrespectful?" Sarah knew this time how childish she sounded. She also knew the answer, but wanted to hear it from her husband.

"Yes, my little sweetheart, without a doubt. We both know how it has benefited us and how calm an atmosphere we have because of it. I will be fair with you and hope you are the same with me. And yes, if I see a reason, you will placed over my knee."

"So you are not cross with me, Daddy?" Sarah asked, no longer crying, barely able to look him in the eye.

"Of course not, my young girl. I was. Now you've been punished and are clearly sorry for how you behaved, I am not. I do forgive you, my sweet." He kissed her forehead.

"Thank you, Daddy." Sarah closed her eyes and enjoyed the closeness felt by them both.

After another ten minutes of holding, both feeling tired, they fell asleep.

Not waking for nearly two hours, Sarah was first to do so for a change. As she moved to glance at the clock on his side table beside the bed, she accidentally woke her husband. It came as a surprise to them both that the spanking spent so much of their energy.

Jack decided it was time to take a walk. "I start work again in two weeks, and before I do, I would love nothing more than to start taking those Sunday walks we used to enjoy so much. I'll enjoy a nice walk through the park and all around town with you, so freshen yourself, and then I will do the same." He lightly smacked Sarah's bottom.

"*Yes, Daddy.*" She quickly moved, happy to be the obedient wife she should have been the entire time.

Whilst walking through the park, linking her arm with Jack's as he held his hands in his pocket, Sarah smiled at people she knew with a feeling of pride. *This is my man. My husband... my Daddy... my hero.* Jack was a war hero; on a more personal level, he was more than that.

Feeling happier than when they both first met, and more than she had ever been in her life, she could say that he was finally his old self again, with that all-important strict disciplinarian step further.

It was a bright day. Although a little cold, the brightness matched her mood. Her bottom was still throbbing, and a part of her wanted to rub it a little, only doing so when nobody was in sight. The throbbing was a good reminder of her place. This made her look at her husband more adoringly than ever. He was the *man* in their marriage and head of their home. If she dared step out of line, her Daddy would not hesitate to put her back in her place.

"Um, you won't tell anyone that you put me over your knee?" If anyone knew that she enjoyed a little spanking for fun, it was not so bad, but for others to know that he spanked her for discipline, for some reason seemed a whole lot worse and humiliating, even if well deserved. "Or..." *Heaven forbid*, she thought, pausing for a moment with dread. "Smack me in front of people?" Sarah was not able completely to look her husband as she asked the latter.

"Tell anyone? Well, I feel there won't be a need for that. After all, you are my wife, and it is not anyone else's business whether I choose to smack your bottom or not. Nor is it any of their business to know any details. Rest assured, my little sweetheart, that I am very unlikely to do such a thing."

"Thank you," she said, feeling somewhat relieved. "But what about..."

"I was just getting to that, little one. It would depend."

"Depend?" Sarah rushed out, "What do you mean, depend?"

"It means, my young girl, it depends on your behaviour. If you are disrespectful to me in public, then yes, there is a strong chance I may. I would give you a proper tanning when we got home, of course. Nevertheless, yes, I may give your bottom a single good smack under such a circumstance. I know that you feel a smacked bottom isn't a smacked bottom unless it's on the bare, but you can trust that that's what you would get when we got home. I may even decide to bare your bottom in public and properly discipline you, there and then. So, my young girl, it would be best that you do not misbehave in public." Jack knew it would be most unlikely for him to smack his wife's bare bottom in public. Still, he knew there was a need to put the threat in place.

Sarah felt a combination of being pleased that her Daddy would go so far... *And be a real man*, she thought, but was also shocked and horrified that anyone would know. A single smack is nothing and not worth worrying about; her Daddy spanking her bare bottom, over his knee in public clearly was a thing to avoid. Sarah knew she would not dare do anything to earn one. She hoped.

In addition, the spanking she would receive arriving home would be much worse. If ever faced with such situation where she had behaved so badly, warranting such, she would do some serious pleading, even be prepared to find a cane, and receive that at home; she would rather that than have him bare her bottom in public, let alone spank her at the same time. That would be something she would use in reserve. With hope, it would not come to that.

"Yes, Daddy," she said, leaning more into him, squeezing his arm.

When Sarah had woken, she was happy to make the tea for them that morning. Not dressing at all, she thought it best that her husband give her permission first. "Until you feel, Daddy, that I have earned the right to wear any clothing, I will refrain from dressing," she said, meekly lowering her head, but enough to make eye contact with her husband. She then left their bedroom, giving her bottom a good rub as she walked down the stairs.

She is so adorable, Jack thought. Her deeply reddened bottom looked so cute.

Jack closed his eyes for a moment, thinking of the week that followed their walk in the park. That Sunday had proved an example of good things to come. They both knew their place and were more than satisfied with it being such a way. It felt natural; the way it should always have been.

Jack and Sarah were up early the following Sunday morning eating breakfast. Jack was reading the paper and talking about what it had to report. When they had finished the current topic, Sarah asked for permission to leave the table.

"Is everything all right, sweetheart?" Jack asked, his curiosity rising. "You've barely touched your breakfast."

"I'm not so sure, Daddy," answered Sarah. "May I be excused?" She asked, nervously.

"Of course," he said, wondering what was troubling her.

Sarah left the dining room and went into the kitchen. A few minutes later, she returned, having removed her clothes, and sat opposite Jack.

Clearly surprised, but enjoying his wife's wonderful petite shaped body, he queried, "Sweetheart?"

"Daddy, I have something to confess." Nervously, Sarah rushed out her next sentence before Jack could leap to any conclusion, "Don't be cross with me, please... I wouldn... I couldn't."

Intrigued and waiting for something he did not want to hear, Jack kept a flat tone to his voice, but was unable to alter the frowned, piercing look upon his face. "Do continue."

"While you were away... I, er, began to feel attracted to..."

"What!" Unable to keep a neutral voice any longer and for a moment forgetting to breathe, his face turned red and eyes became more piercing.

A strong need to talk at a more fast pace became apparent. "No, no, no... It's not like that. I didn't do anything. I began to...couldn't do... didn't do anything, I promise, Daddy, I swear!" Sarah began to breathe heavier, gripping the sides of her thighs, left hand still holding the wooden spoon, feeling more and more nervous and frightened.

Allowing his wife to continue, he let go of his breath and sighed a relief. He had often wondered whilst away whether Sarah was unfaithful. He had known people that received the infamous *Dear John* letter, and no doubt, others were in an unenviable position of never knowing that their wives had been unfaithful. *Or perhaps not knowing was for the best, I don't know.*

Sarah was being honest. That was one of the many reasons he loved her. If she was attracted to someone else, it was nothing. *Well, not quite nothing, though it happens.* If she had done the unthinkable, it would obviously be another matter.

Relieved to see her husband's sigh of relief, Sarah found her normal breath and continued, "With the shortages and rationing, and then the Yanks arriving, they had much to give when we had little.

"They were charming, well dressed and friendly. One of them had a real liking for me. He gave me stockings and certain foods I could not get hold of nor had seen in a while. He was attractive and had much to offer... but was not you, my love. He wasn't you... *my Daddy*." She paused for a moment before holding out the wooden spoon he had used before to discipline her. "I want you to take this and use it appropriately. I feel so guilty for those feelings and need to be punished."

Jack was ready to discipline his wife, but of course understood her predicament. He wanted to re-assure her, "You will be punished, my young one, but I do understand why you would have felt that way. I am well aware of the phrase *'Over paid, over dressed and over here!'*"

"Um, Daddy, isn't that *'Over dressed, over sexed and over here!'*?"

Jack raised an eyebrow knowing she was correct. Sarah lowered her head completely and hugged the wooden spoon. She could not bring herself to look him in the eyes.

"Very true, young one. But before I use that wooden

spoon, I need to let you know something that happened on my way home. Look up, sweetheart."

"Yes, Daddy." She slowly obeyed him.

"Of course, our nation is grateful for the American assistance and then their much-needed alliance during the war. After all, we could not have won it without them. However, I do remember a brief argument with one American who doubted the importance of our country's role in the victory. I stated, determined to be brief, that we were in it from the start, and if we had surrendered, especially earlier in the war, I would have reunited with my beloved wife a lot sooner. Moreover, Italy would not have switched sides nor would other countries have had the chance to follow suit; European and African resources would belong mostly to the Nazis for a start; and the Soviets would have been in serious peril. Not to mention what would have happened in the Far East. In addition, try a D-Day launch from the east coast of America…"

To this last part, being in so much trouble, Sarah felt chagrined when she gave tiny laugh; beginning to smile, she suddenly stopped herself.

"But that was one American. The others I got on with very well, sweetheart. And do laugh. You will be punished as you request, but no, I am not as cross with you, as you may think.

"Why mention that man, sweetheart, you may wonder? I do so, because I believe he was disgruntled at not succeeding with a certain girl… you."

Sarah turned pale, her eyes widened; her mouth opened a little before she closed it sharply. She was not sure of where to look. She could not speak. Lowering her head, again, seemed the safest option.

Allowing her to do so, Jack explained, "On my way home, I had to make a change-over or two. While I was waiting, I was drinking some tea in a near by coffee bar -I still prefer tea, sweetheart- when I overheard an unhappy GI who decided to criticise, stupidly, the British war effort. I defended in the manner I spoke of, and would see where he wanted to take the issue.

"He stormed off, to return not long after, with an apology. He became very diplomatic, wanting to show that he was an intelligent fellow, in spite of his recent comments.

"We had a good conversation about the war and other issues; most notable of all was you, young one.

"To start, he praised our country and the British Empire for its invaluable service, and more.

"I was in no hurry to correct him when he rightly affirmed that we needed each other and that victory would not have been possible otherwise. What surprised me was perhaps his genuine wisdom once he had calmed down somewhat, was that he recognised everyone who did their bit. Civilians and armed force members of the combined Allied forces I had expected, but also all others who opposed the Axis powers.

"These included those occupied countries with resistance armies; to the countries that once allied themselves with the Nazis, for one reason or another, switched sides. He even acknowledged those Germans who resisted their Nazi leaders, and the German Resistance in particular of those from that country whom, even though relatively small in number, on occasions, attempted to assassinate Hitler, sadly failing and consequently paying a heavy price. With their failure, we all paid a very heavy price.

"Of course mind you, sweetheart, if we had listened to Churchill prior to war and before he became Prime Minister, along with those holding similar opinions; had we confronted the Nazis before they got any stronger, instead of appeasing them, you can't help but feel how better off we all would have been. That, my little sweetheart, is something we cannot do anything about.

"Your behaviour, although not quite the same analogy, I'm glad I did not appease for much longer. I would not like to think how worse off our lives would have been."

Sarah gently nodded her head in agreement. She still could not bring herself to look her Daddy in the eyes or even talk. She would only look down upon the floor and keep quiet, deciding that she may as well get used to looking at the floor. As for her silence, she knew it would not last much longer.

"Anyway, back to this Yank fella. He convinced me to try a coffee, which wasn't as bad as I thought. We played a few games of cards before catching trains in opposite directions. It was during those games that, although I lost money, discovered I had not lost a wife. He told me he had fallen for a very pretty girl. To my amazement, it was you.

"He tried to win you over in the manner you told me. Even with his charm, ignoring the one that emerged when I first met him, you were determined to remain faithful. For that I am very proud of you, my little sweetheart."

Sarah slowly matched his eyes; she smiled, feeling herself blush.

"When he told me about a certain girl, I didn't know what to do. He told me he would like to have seen the man to whom she was so devoted. If he had succeeded with you, in any way, I would have reacted differently. As tempted I was, I did not tell him my full name. He was too upset to ask. I pointed to behind me, where he noticed two girls. I had spotted them earlier. One of them had noticed his uniform and seemed shyly attracted to him. I told him, 'what a better way to get over this girl.' My eyes then directed him towards them.

"He wisely agreed. Without wasting any time, he began

talking to this highly attractive girl.

"My train shortly arrived. It was then my thoughts returned to you. I was still nervous at the thought of reuniting with you. I had no idea whether you would feel the same when you actually saw me again."

"I…" She found herself able to speak, if only just, "I was dreading the same, Daddy. But why didn't you tell me?"

"I wanted to hear it from you. I knew it was only a matter of time. Contrary to how you really felt, until I took you in hand, I did at one point wonder whether you had had a change of heart. Things fortunately fell into place. In a way, you were feeling neglected by me not being strict with you. As I said, things had fortunately fallen into place."

"I am sorry, Daddy," she said in a quiet tone.

"You are forgiven, my little sweetheart. Being far away from you, and knowing of the shortages back home and the air raids, followed in time by the arrival of the Yanks, and with what they could offer, I was worried. After all, their reputation with the women was well known. He tried, like many others, I am sure… but you refused them. Even if mildly attracted to him, after too long alone and needing a man around, you still waited for me. Letting you know, although good looking girls were around, my only desires laid with you." He pulled out his chair a little and patted his lap.

"Thank you, Daddy." Sarah smiled happily before feeling a level of guilt she knew would only find its cure by spending a deserved amount of time over his knee.

She rose from her seat, and with a pouting expression, moved towards Jack. She gave him the wooden spoon, and gently laid herself gently over his lap. "Sorry, Daddy."

Jack altered his wife's position so both of them were more comfortable. He caressed her cute little bottom.

All I want to do is sit you on my knee, my little girl, and give you a damn good cuddle. That will come later, he thought. For now, she needed him to be a strict loving husband and Daddy, and provide her with the discipline she needed. "You will find it very hard to sit for days, my little sweetheart."

"Yes, Daddy." She spoke barely a whisper; that, they both knew, would swiftly change.

Jack swapped the implement from his left to right hand and held Sarah securely with his left, resting the wooden spoon against his wife's cute little bottom for aim; he cleared his throat before raising his arm...

His little sweetheart gasped...

Spanko Or Not A Spanko?
~Brat No. 7: Heather~

It began more or less as a dare. That is, on the surface, how it appeared. In truth, it was a well-calculated set of circumstances in order to find out whether a certain girl was a spanko.

Love can be a very strange thing. A person may work with a girl for best part of a year; all the while not feeling anything. Then in the next moment, like a clichéd lightning strike, a feeling much greater than once thought possible occurs.

This is what happened to Scott. He was a tall, good looking, blue-eyed and fair-headed man entering his mid twenties.

When it came to girls, he was very fussy. He had an idea of the type of girl he wanted, and as it happens, this certain girl had most of what he was looking for. There was one thing though that remained undiscovered.

Scott, known to his friends as Scottie, included a certain girl at work by the name of Heather, whom parenthetically, he struggled to keep his eyes away from while on his lunch break on a fine Five-Past-Twelve mid-day, Friday in April.

Ah, a nice day for change, so no shock really to find outside, several people... you included, Heather. Heather, Heather, Heather, he thought with a sigh.

Heather was there, too; her hair, annoyingly attractive, found itself blown and flowing slightly in the cool breeze.

It bloody well would be. Shouldn't swear, even mildly. Should set a better example. I wouldn't spank her for using that word, say she ever used it in an inappropriate manner. He looked at her irresistibly spankable bottom... *Yes, I would.*

My friends don't know, and certainly neither do you, that I'm a spanko. What to do? Ah, Scottie, Scottie, Scottie, he thought, again with a sigh. *Scottie doesn't know...* He laughed – a private joke regarding his mobile phone ring tune. *I need to know. I must find out. Are you, Heather, a spanko? On the other hand... -at least one of them smacking your bottom, oh come on!- ... you have a little interest, and along with it, are curious enough for the potential to unleash it. I have an idea, and only one way to find out.*

Heather was just below average height, had large hazel eyes and reddish hair that flowed to around her shoulders, which if she chose was straight or left untouched resulted in wavy hair, both Scottie found attractive in its own way. Interestingly enough it did have in parts a touch of blonde, but not much at all... *Yet you prefer to say strawberry-blonde, which it was not... or perhaps it was. Red hair basically, but such a conversation would be best with you across my knee.*

Scottie had noticed a few things about her, but they never

seemed as cute as they did at this moment. One of which was that she had a tiny nose. Another, the look on her face when she was lost in thought. She would purse her lips and twist her mouth to the left or right, sometimes with a frown or a simple expression on her face clearly showing that she was lost in thought.

There was more to Heather than her outer appearance that drove him wild; there was that fun side to her personality; how cute of how she would sound without trying. Wittiness and cheekiness seemed to radiate from her. Heather certainly had a little brat inside her, but still, she was a nice girl. She could be a little too sensitive at times. *That,* Scottie thought, *is hardly an issue... I want to be there to comfort you. You do have your moody moments, but yet again, this is hardly a problem, as everyone, especially girls, have such moments from time to time.*

Another thing Scottie had always found attractive was that she never used bad language. For a male spanko to find a girl like this, it would naturally have its pluses and minuses. It was an added lady-like manner much appreciated. After all, a horribly foul-mouthed girl would not compliment her good looks. If she would swear a little and need a smacked bottom as a reminder not to use such language in future, would be fine, and for a spanko, perhaps best. Still, Scottie was sure there would be plenty of things she would do to warrant a need for a spanking.

Heather had turned eighteen a few months before. She would soon finish college and return to work for the summer. Scottie had not seen her for nearly a year. He was not sure as to what happened in that year, but he had noticed the changes in her. Last year there would have been particular actions that if he or anyone else had taken, she would view it as patronising or the like, and not like it. Even if meant with affection, she would still dislike it. Suddenly, that all changed.

Whatever had happened in that year, she had grown into the woman she wanted to be; alternatively, and most likely, she was beginning to find the woman in herself that she wanted to become.

Was such a woman a girl...oh, such an awesome girl... wherein a good spanking is hankered for?

The answer came to Scottie a lot faster than he expected.

Fortunately, Scottie had an easy day ahead with a small amount of paperwork. It was well timed. Scottie had no intention of working. If needed, he would pretend to be unwell. It seldom occurred, but after all, *people do become sick*, he thought. He was. *I am. Oh, good Spirits, I am! I'm sick of putting my hand across your bottom, little girl, and not knowing whether you truly like it or not.*

Heather enjoyed it when Scottie lifted her and put her over his shoulder. That was certain. Her bottom exposed up there, it was too hard to resist.

He remembered two weeks earlier when he first smacked her bottom whilst over his shoulder. Energy wanting to burst out of him and repeat the action happened every time. He had done this about half a dozen times. She had such a spankable bottom. *It felt sooo good. Why is it I can think of nothing else?*

Heather was in his office area doing something or other. She giggled about something. She looked so cute. And then she turned around... *There's my answer.* He gritted and grinded his teeth for a moment.

She liked it. She must. Yet was it a case of her enjoying the smacked bottom, but not me? Scottie had to act, and act soon. It was tricky. Heather had a boyfriend, but it appeared as if she was dissatisfied.

Scottie had tested her. "As long as he is satisfying you in the way you wish..." Heather responded with a quiet grunt, hardly heard, but spoke loud and clear.

Another test would decide the next course of action. On their lunch break, he started a conversation; Heather began behaving a little silly, when on the radio, she heard one of her favourite songs.

You are cute, my little Heather, including your funky dance, I'll give you that.

She had had a burst of energy from the caffeine in her coffee.

That, along with the music from the radio, no doubt, has certainly boosted your energy levels... Level? ... Levels? ... Whatever... Imagine such energy when... He snapped himself out of his trance. *It's time.*

His planned conversation would be out of earshot.

Before anyone came over, Scottie made sure that in the next few minutes, either one way or the other, he would know whether Heather was a spanko or not.

She was still performing her little dance. "As cute as that is, you should try calming yourself." Scottie told her with a light laugh.

"Why?" Heather asked as she stopped for a moment.

"Have you ever seen *Austin Powers*?"

"I love *Austin Powers*." Her interest in dancing waned as she pick up her mug of coffee, ready to talk about *Austin Powers*, sipping happily away through a straw.

An added cuteness it is, that straw thing, little one.

"Well," he said. *I may as well get straight to it.* "You know what he says regarding smacked bottoms, don't you?" Scottie coughed and prepared his best vocal impersonation.

His performance was pretty convincing.

Heather giggled. "Go on, then."

With an eyebrow raised, he said, "OooKay... Well, slightly different from *Austin Powers*, I will be careful as to who knows. I will carry you home. And, as you lay over my shoulder, we will discuss a few things. One of which, little Heather, is you biting your fingernails."

"I can't stop," she said with honesty.

"Well, we will soon see about that," Scottie told her, mildly laughing.

She's not joking either, whether biting her fingernails or the dare to spank her. As for the fingernail biting, I will make you stop, little Heather. A good smacked bottom, and plenty of them, will sort that out. But, and thank the Spirit World, she is a spanko. I hope.

I will put you over my knee as soon as I get you back to your place, my girl.

Just as their conversation had finished, it was time to get back to work.

And so, after his break, he sat at his desk. He leaned back.

Oh, there is no chance of me getting any work done today.

The working day wound down so slow. Scottie's thoughts were on what he would do with Heather. It was certain that what she needed was a good spanking.

As far as Scottie was concerned, after what seemed longer that a few weeks, he would finally have her over his knee.

After work, Scottie and Heather met outside. "Let's walk to that point first, little one."

Heather agreed as she walked beside him.

No sooner had they turned the corner, Scottie lifted Heather and put her over his shoulder. The expected giggle from Heather sounded so cute. She let out another giggle as Scottie's hand smacked across her bottom.

"Right, young lady. There are several things to talk about. One of which, your hair is beautiful."

"Ow! What was that for?"

"I can't see, but I know you just rolled your eyes, little one. Your hair is beautiful. Is it not?"

"It is n-Ow! Fine. It is. But, it's not. Ow!"

"I can do this all day, little Heather."

"Okay... fine!" Heather began sounding like the little brat she really was. "It is," she said... *Not*, she thought.

"Good girl." Scottie patted her bottom. He could not wait to spank her bare bottom; he would not rush the spanking straight to that part, as much as part of him wanted to.

It did not take more than ten minutes before they approached her home. She still lived with her parents, but fortunately, they were away for a few days. He put her down and she unlocked the door.

They entered, and whilst Heather locked the door, Scottie looked around and complimented her home. "Very nice home you have here. There is one little thing I would recommend. Not about the home, but referring to those." He pointed to the window. "Purely up to you, but you might wanna close those blinds. That is unless, of course, you want anyone who may walk passed to glance in and see what's happening."

Heather gave him a *Well, obviously* look that told him she did not want the entire world, or anyone who walked passed the window, to witness Scottie spanking her.

"Well, you may. And by the way, for that look, I am gonna spank you much harder, little girl."

She flashed her tongue at him.

"Ooh, that does it. Just you wait till you are over my knee." Instead of worrying her, his threatening words made her smile. *Such a cute, mischievous smile you have, my little Heather,* he thought.

With the door locked, Heather walked straight over to the window to close the blinds. She followed this up by checking and shutting all the windows in the house.

Scottie waited impatiently with an outward expression of patience.

When Heather returned to the room, taking hold of her arm, he pulled her close. Scottie proceeded to lift her, scooping up her legs. She lay horizontally with his left arm holding her up below her stomach. His right arm held her below her legs.

The following thirty minutes passed as a blur. Time became what it seemed in slow motion as Scottie sat and put Heather across his lap. She let out a cute gasp as he initially lifted her. She let out another gasp as she lay for the first time across his knee.

The blur continued as Scottie's hand smacked across her trousered bottom. The material felt so good; he imagined it felt good for Heather, too.

Smack followed smack as his hand refused to neglect either cheek. Time had sped during parts of the spanking, but still a constant blur. He caressed her bottom in between a hailstorm that was his hand smacking her clothed bottom.

The time had come to take it further... at last.

Scottie tugged down Heather's trousers revealing his first glance at parts of her bare, and soon to be fully naked, bottom.

Fighting the urge to rip down her panties, his hand, time still a blur, began again to rain down upon such beautiful, partly covered, cheeks.

The primeval grunts that came from Heather were proof that she was not only enjoying the spanking, but also had been in need of one for some time.

Without a doubt, and very much so, she enjoyed lying face down over Scottie's lap. Avoiding his hand landing across her bottom did not enter her mind, in fact the opposite, as she raised her bottom wanting to meet his large hand.

Continuing to moan, she went back and forth from an aggressive grunt to a cute yelp. Each was a pleasurable sound to Scottie's ears.

Time came for what he had wanted all along. He could not resist any further. The fact he had done so, so far, took him by surprise.

Her cute looking panties, with ice cream cones and teddy bears, were soon to be protection no more for her bottom.

Still going against the grain, he peeled them down unveiling her beautiful bottom, made even more so with the desired effect of the spanking thus far. It felt like heaven for his hand to caress its warm surface.

With a steady pace, just as before, his hand, like heavy rain, came down upon her cheeks. Her bottom bounced as if raindrops pounding the surface recoiled from such a force.

She made her bottom rise in want of more and more of Scottie's hand, predicting the moment of heavenly contact.

Noticing this pattern, he alternated his speed and flow, in order to make it less predictable.

He could not read her thoughts, but it was obvious she was enjoying this, and just as much as he was.

Feeling her increasingly reddened and heated bottom was a moment, and one in which the wait felt longer, that Scottie had so hungered for.

Although not from him, but now unbelievably happy it was, Heather had been hankering, ever so much so, as Scottie had once wondered, for a firm hand to smack hard across her bottom.

While the spanking continued, it marked the start of

their relationship. A relationship that Scottie and Heather both found most satisfying.

Growing up, Heather's parents never spanked her, but she had almost always been fascinated with spanking. Talking about it to anyone was too embarrassing a thought; she was too scared to mention it to any of her previous boyfriends, including her soon to be ex-boyfriend, in case they looked upon her as weird. Fortunately, that was a problem no more.

In Scottie's mind, the lingering question concerning Heather was **Spanko** *or not a spanko?* *To his great relief and now pleasure, the answer was abundantly clear.*

They were perfect for one another; always will be.

They enjoyed their Saturday night out with their friends. This was in spite of Heather giving Scottie a little attitude; he made her slow down her drinking, which did not please her. She drank a lot more than she would normally, and Scottie knew this and the affect it would have on her throughout the course of the next day.

Not wanting it to ruin the night, for themselves or their friends, he told her quietly but firmly, "We will *discuss* this in the morning, little girl."

"Sure, sure, sure," was her response. Heather was too drunk to care. Nevertheless, the warning of what was to come did make her behave for the remainder of the night.

Since she was sleeping at his home that night, she had hoped the alcohol making him forget.

She did enjoy sleeping at Scottie's home, and had done so frequently. Unfortunately, the main draw back with this was that any *discussion* in the morning became that much easier.

They had been together for nine weeks. Scottie felt as if he was the happiest man in the world, and Heather, al-

though equally happy, was not a happy bunny that morning; hangovers being their usual annoying selves.

Heather knew what he would do, and even though that was normally what she wanted, with her hangover, such discipline, she hoped, could wait.

"Morning, little one." Scottie was not suffering from a hangover, choosing his drink wisely, was able to drink a lot and still feel good in the morning. Besides, he wanted to remain in control considering he needed to make sure he was capable of looking after not only himself, but Heather as well.

"Morn." Heather rubbed her eyes and groaned. "I feel like crap." *Crap* was as close she came to swearing.

"Come here, you." Scottie's tone was deceptively kind. Heather walked up to him, thinking he was going to give her a typical morning hug; instead, he swiped his hand across her bottom. "I will not have you saying that."

"'Hey! *Crap* is not a swear word." No sooner had she finished speaking, Scottie's hand swiftly came across her bottom again. "Fine!" she relented.

"I take that as an agreement with my view. Although it's not a bad swear word, I will not have you using it unless you want more. And don't you dare think of saying it again or repeating it to get another smack; you are in enough trouble as it is."

"How so? Oh, Cr... Oh," she stopped talking and pursed her lips together. She remembered being cheeky, but that was her nature. Thinking it best to be cute, she said, "But I was drunk. We all do things we shouldn't. After all, I danced with you... or at least I think it was you," she said, then exaggerated her face as she pretended to rack her brains; a moment later, she could not hold back her naughty little giggle.

You are very cute, little one... Not the point, he thought.

He could not help but smile, but purposely changed his countenance. "Now is not the time for humour, little one. I will not have you giving me that attitude. We needed to go home, and as fun as it was putting you over my shoulder again, and as much as you enjoyed it, that is not the point."

…… Crap. I forgot I gave a little attitude, she thought. *When the nightclub closed… it was only a little. Yes, it was four in the morning, but there were other places that opened till six. I was beginning to get sleepy. Not the point.*

"Then what is?" Heather exaggerated her words as she raised her hands and outstretched her arms.

"The attitude you gave me, little girl." Scottie was becoming increasingly annoyed. "You still haven't apologised. All you've done is try to be cute, and granted, you have been that, but it will only end with a very sore bottom. But since you have a hangover, I will wait before spanking you."

"Don't I have a say in any of this?" Heather knew the answer; however, she wanted to push her luck as far as she could.

"You do not, my girl," Scottie said, flatly.

"Well, it's not gonna happen now, so…" She flashed her tongue.

"I was not intending to blow this out of proportion, but just so I know, do you intend on saying sorry for how you behaved last night?"

Heather exhaled and rolled her eyes. "Okay now. You maaay have a point. You maaay be right, but still, I don't have anything to be sorry for. So drop it before you stress yourself out over it. I need some tabletie-whatsits." She walked slowly towards the cupboard and search for some.

Scottie reached out his hand and stopped her. "You will not be getting any until we have finished talking, little one."

"Then stop talking and I'll be free to get some." She

tried to move, but Scottie held firmly onto her arm.

Fast approaching a stage where he was having no more of her cheek, Scottie gave Heather a final warning. "This is the last straw, little girl."

"Straws? We had straws? *I want straws*. If you have the last one, go to the shop you silly man and get some. Whilst you're at it, get some more tabletie-things, I think we're running low on those, too." She smiled, impressed at her cheekiness, even when slightly hung-over.

"You..." Scottie gave Heather a solid smack across her bottom causing her to yelp out much louder than she expected. As she began rubbing her bottom with her right hand, he dragged her with his left. "I've changed my mind, little girl. You're getting it, right now!"

"All right, okay, I'm sorry." Heather wanted to push her luck as far as she could, but even so, she certainly disliked the thought of pushing her luck beyond what was acceptable and receive a sore bottom along with her already sore head.

"Too late, my girl. I gave you plenty of chances and you chose not to take them. Soon I'll have you apologising in no time."

Scottie sat on one of the high stools near the kitchen side-table not too far away from the main kitchen table, and with an almost effortlessness, he grabbed Heather by the waist, lifted her and put her over his knee.

Admiring how cute she looked as her legs and hands dangled, and her bottom nicely on display at the perfect angle, he felt himself go hard as the tight shorts she wore for bed complimented her well-shaped bottom. Caressing it before raising his arm, he scolded, "I would have rather done this later when your head felt somewhat better, but you leave me with no choice."

"What if I said I'm sorry now, would it change things?" Heather figured it was worth a shot.

"No, it would not, my girl. But if you do say so, though, it may not be as long."

"But you're still gonna spank me, so in that case, I won't. Maybe at the end... dependi-Ouch!"

Scottie was not going to hear any more of her cheek and his hand came cracking down upon her bottom. "That's enough out of you." He began and maintained a steady pace, but would make sure the spanking was not over with too quickly.

The cotton material felt good against his hand. It was always a pleasure to spank his little brat's bottom, and the material along with the tightness made it feel even better. He also knew that due to the tightness, the heat produced from the spanking would keep it within and make it more painful. That, after all, was what his little brat needed.

Heather tried in vain to reach her arm back and cover her bottom as Scottie took a firm hold, putting it against her back. "For that, my girl," he scolded, continuing to spank her around the same pace. "I will spank you even longer. There is no chance of you preventing this."

"I'm sorry," she cried out.

"I know you are sorry now, my girl. You'll be even sorrier b'time I'm through with you." A pleasure as always to spank, Scottie was very cross with Heather and going to teach her a lesson. "It's easy to say sorry when you are being spanked. Next time when you behave in such a way, I hope there will not even be a need to spank you about apologising. You should come to me and willingly do so."

"Ow! Ow! Ow! Ow! Ow! Yes-Ow!" The pain in Heather's head had almost disappeared. All she could feel was the burning sting from her bottom. She was beginning to regret behaving like such a brat.

She loved her tight shorts, but those same tight shorts became a source of regret at such a moment. *Another one,* she thought.

"I mean it, little one. There has to be a stop point when you are so cheeky. I should not have to even mention spankings. As I have told you many times, you're cheekiness and playful nature is one of the things I most love you for." Scottie paused.

He realised in that moment he had never added *love* in such a sentence. It was clear enough for him that he was falling in love, more truthfully, he was in love, but had not said so. It became suddenly so strange. He thought he would have said so by now. Caressing her bottom feeling the heat, he cleared his throat and began to spank once again. "But still, there is a time to stop, and unless you don't learn, there will be many more spankings in your future. Is this clear, little one?" He stopped to hear her answer.

Already losing her breath, Heather asked, "Did you just say you loved me?"

"Er, yes. That is not the point, little girl. Nor the answer I am expecting."

"It *is* the point. You did, didn't you?"

"Yes." Scottie exhaled a sigh. "I do. I am head over heals in love with you. Because I love you so much, I will be stricter with you. Even if you try to behave, I know you'll do plenty of naughty things, which even may be cute will still earn you a damn good spanking. Oh yes, and to let you know, my little girl, I am not through with you." Trying to move on from what he said, he realised a ramble of a sentence he just spoke. He was in love and he had finally said so.

Even though her bottom was becoming sore along with her head, which was, interestingly enough, feeling a little better, but still not as it should, Heather had huge smile on her face. She knew that would soon change when Scottie continued, but for that moment, she cared not. She had been waiting to hear those words, and an extreme feeling of joy filled her. "Yes, sir, I will try. But you know what I'm like."

Scottie gave a single hard smack that caught Heather by surprise; she gave a cute yelp.

"Yes, I do, little one. That is why I love you so much. Now stop distracting me. You have been very naughty," he scolded, trying to focus more on smacking his impudent little girl.

"Wait!" Heather called out.

"You are making this last even longer, little one. I would have thought you would want this over with, what with your hangover." He still found her very cute and was more than happy to prolong her punishment.

"What if I said I loved you, too? Would that not make you want to stop?" She hoped that those words would help her out of her predicament. She was in love, but wanted to wait until Scottie had told her first, which he had just done. She could reply in kind any time. That made her happy. If she could use it to get out of a spanking earlier, it was worth a shot. "Then, maybe if you want to, later you can spank me."

Scottie suspected that she loved him. He still wanted to hear those words from her. "I most likely will spank you later, little one, depending on your behaviour. But no, it would not make me stop."

"Hmph! Then I won't say it!"

"That does it, you!" He made a purpose to spank much harder this time and did so rapidly causing the desired effect of *Owie's* from Heather. He stopped spanking for a moment, but only to lower her shorts.

Intending to peel down her shorts slowly, it was a pleasant surprise when her bottom popped out in the open faster than he expected. Scottie held himself back from rubbing such a beautifully shaped bottom. Heather would no doubt appreciate it greatly as much as he would enjoy it, but this was a punishment. Heather exhaled a satisfied sigh of relief as the cool air in the kitchen gave a tiny relief to her burning bottom.

"Pleeeease, sir. Rub my bottom. It burns and stings," she said, childishly.

"No, little one, I will not. Later, yes. But not while you are being disciplined." Scottie was firm, albeit going against the grain.

"You did a little earlier. Why not now? You know you'd enjoy it." Heather lifted herself by holding the seat of the high stool and Scottie's lap. She turned her head trying to look at Scottie's face. He flashed her smile before shaking his head. Disappointed and feeling moody at not being able to manipulate him, she growled and added, "Fine!" Heather wanted very much to punch Scottie's calf, but knew that would be a stupid thing to do. All she could do was allow her hands and upper body to dangle, and look down upon the floor again.

"No, little girl." Scottie pulled down her shorts even further. As he was about to continue to spank, but on Heather's bare bottom, he felt a sharp blow to his calf which nearly put him off balance and could have resulted in Heather falling off his lap. "That does it you little brat!" Scottie was furious. His hand came down hard and fast, cracking against her tender pinkish-reddened skin making it bounce and wobble in a constant motion as he smacked her bottom non-stop. "Do you even know how dangerous that was? You could have easily hit your head on the floor. I can't believe you acted in such a thoughtless manner, my girl!"

"Ow! Ow! Ow! Ah! Ooh! Ah! Ow! Ow! Ooh! Ooh!

Ooh! Ooh!!!!" Heather gasped for air. "I'm soooooorrrry-yyy! I... Ow! Ow! Don't-Ow! Know-Ah! Ah!" she cried out before sucking in more air through gritted teeth, and continuing, "what came over me! Ooh! Ooh! Ooh!!"

"I do. I believe *brat* has something to do with it, and something that will be dealt with accordingly!" Scottie was keeping up with his new harder and faster pace causing Heather to kick her legs and hold on to the legs of the high stool with a firm grip.

Whilst trying to take deep breaths when it was possible, she tried to apologise, but could not get the words out.

Heather was again regretting her behaviour. When she was able to think of anything but the pain and sting, which was on the increase spreading across her bottom, things became clear; she would need to think more about the consequences of her actions. It seemed obvious, but amazingly took several spankings and this current serious one to realise that. Although, she knew, she would most likely forget and end up in the same position.

A fortunate thing for her was that she had a high pain threshold for spankings; her bottom, though highly cute, was a tough bottom at that, and thus did not bruise easily. She knew this did not work in her favour when it came to disciplinary spankings.

This time it was different. Heather felt every hard thwack that smacked across her bottom. This was, by far, the hardest spanking she had ever received.

Whilst Scottie's hand was bouncing hard and fast off his little brat's bottom, the sound cracking loud around the kitchen, her bare flesh was beginning to glow even brighter.

He decided to slow down. "I am hoping this will teach you a lesson that will be remembered, little girl." He spotted a plastic spatula on the side. Stopping to test whether he could reach it, Heather looked up.

Out of breath, she asked, "What are you doing? What are you reaching for?" Heather saw Scottie grab hold of the plastic spatula. Sharply inhaling with eyes widened, she cried out desperately, "Nooo! Please, not that!"

She continued to beg, remembering one time when she and Scottie first were seeing one another, how he playfully whacked her bottom with it. She had a high pain threshold for the hand, but not, to her displeasure, hard plastic. Scottie had only spanked with his hand, and she prayed he would not use a plastic hairbrush or worse, a bath brush... *This would be painful enough!* "I'm sorry, I'm sorry, please! I'll be good, I'll be good!"

Suddenly, Scottie's phone rang.

"What... You stay there, little one." Scottie tapped her bottom before reaching out to pick it up.

"I'm not going anywhere... Sorry-Ow!" Heather decided she must work on thinking before she spoke. She could not help grinning at Scottie's ring tone. It came from the film *Euro Trip*. A comical side to his personality she loved. Especially when he could switch from that at any moment when she misbehaved, becoming old-fashioned strict disciplinarian with her.

"Yo' 'ello, 'ello. All right Franklin, mate, 'ow's things? I mean, Maestro," Scottie said, teasing his old friend; Franklin was know as *the Maestro* for success with the ladies, his tall, dark and handsome appearance combined with the gift of the gab aided him in this.

Heather could only just hear Scottie's friend on the other end of the line, and noticed he spoke a little more properly when conversing with her. She knew he would watch his language around her, but of course, not with his friends. It was rare she heard him swear, except for the time he dropped a box on his foot or got excited about something. Whenever he did, he would allow her a certain amount of heavy brat time spank-free.

"Dude, don't even..." the Maestro mock-warned him, laughing. He then answered, "Pretty sweet. Should tell you 'bout last night. 'Ang on a min. You seem a little out of breath. I hope I 'aven't caught you at the wrong time?" He gave an exaggerated, horrified groan before laughing.

"A little, mate. But it's not quite like that." Scottie laughed. Without thinking, he moved Heather's hand, which had reached back in an attempt to rub her burning bottom; he began petting it himself.

Grateful of the relief and not wanting to remind him he was doing so during a punishment, she lay dangling helplessly over his lap. She remained quiet, additionally not wanting to provoke an automatic smack that Franklyn would hear on the other end of the phone. Heather was certain she did not want him to tell Franklin or any of his other friends, or hers for that matter, that he spanks her. That thought alone horrified her into silence.

"Dude, say no more. I'll leave ya' to it. I'll tell you what; tell you in the pub this Wednesday when we meet for the England game. I'll even tell you twice; once when we get there and again when the lads join us, all right?"

"Cool. Sweet as, mate. See you then."

"Later, mate."

"Right, you..." Scottie said, firmly, speaking to Heather; as much as he would rather not, he stopped petting her bottom. *Amazing, I didn't realise I started to,* he thought.

"Mate?"

"... Shite!" Scottie laughed, more with shock, realising he forgot to end the call properly.

Heather turned her head sharply. Her eyes wide and mouth open. She wanted, in an interesting turn around, to scold him. *You damn foolish... fool! Dammit! Why can't I swear?* she thought, a tad irritated. While Scottie spoke for a minute more, insisting that his mate had not interrupted anything, not convincing the Maestro for one second, she pondered... *Perhaps I was smacked, once perhaps, as a child for swearing, but forgot... hmm. Nah, I'd remember something like that. Besides, be hypocritical, would that. Shall I smack them for every time they swear? Actually, they seldom swear... In any case, my parents take a level of pride in having disciplined me in other ways. Maybe it's just me. Damn well sucks, though! Not really... It's just not me. Still, I think it's Scottie that needs a damn good spanking, not me, for his carelessness! Well, no, not really... Grr! He is ri- not-so-wrong... I am in need of this. He is... not... so... wrong. There! Grr!*

"Dude, dude, dude..." the Maestro said, his tone accentuating his belief of Scottie's abysmal attempt at subterfuge. "While you try convincing yourself, 'cause I'm not, I'll leave ya' to it, 'kay," he said, laughing. Extending the two middle-ish letters, still laughing away, his only departing word was... "Sweet!" He then ended the call.

"Don't you know how to use the phone?" Heather began to scold, overstating her words, "And don't mind me just dangling here. I'll just be twiddling my thumbs, shall-Ow!"

"You be quiet, little girl. He did not hear, and if he had, you'd deserve it. And just to mention it quickly before you do, *shite* is not a swear word." Scottie reached for the spatula that he put down when he picked up his phone. "Are you still comfortable, little one?"

In a much better attempt to think before she spoke, she said in a highly polite manner, "Yes, sir. Except for my bottom, sir."

He grinned, feeling less angry with his girlfriend. He was surprised by her respectful turn-a-round. *You are so damn cute,* he thought. Her cuteness always had a way of making him happy, even if it she was very naughty at the time. If she were to act cute when naughty, it would give him the perfect reason to spank her; or, if already spanking her, smack her ever so lovely bottom some more. "We're nearly finished. In fact, we will only have six more to go, but it will be with the plastic spatula."

With a heavy sigh, Heather accepted his decision, grateful it was only six. "Yes, sir. Thank you, sir."

Scottie pressed the spatula against Heather's bottom for aim and then raised his arm. He swung it hard, creating a different cracking sound to that of his hand, but one that clearly gave the impression, along with Heather's cries, that the spatula was very effective.

"OW! OWW!" Heather cried out much louder than when she was spanked with Scottie's hand. With teary eyes, the pain lingered throughout her already throbbing bottom, which made her cry out in the same manner as if spanked constantly. "Ow! Ow! Ow! Ow! Ow! Ooh, Owie! Owie! Owie!" She inhaled before howling, "Owwwww!!"

"Oh, stop your whining, little one." Scottie's tone was uncharacteristically unsympathetic, believing that Heather was pretending to be in more pain than she really was.

Displeased with his lack of empathy, she cried out, sounding much more childish than she meant, but meaning every word except for the last insult. "You would, too, if you were in my position, you bulbous balloon!"

"What did you just say?!" Scottie brought the spatula down upon Heather's bottom hard and fast.

"YEOW! OW! AHHH!" Heather screamed and began to cry.

Stunned, Scottie had noticed Heather's legs stop kicking and go limp, as did the rest of her body as she cried. He stopped and spoke quietly, "I know I have spanked you harder this time round, but didn't realise the plastic spatula would have that much of an effect. At least I know for the future." He looked down upon a bright red bottom, "I apologise for telling you to stop whining. I thought you were pretending. Just as you have in the past."

Heather spoke softly, but as firm as she could through tears, "Well... I wasn't." She sniffed.

"I make that number five. You have one more, my cute little girl."

"...'Kay." She spoke extremely quiet, agreeing reluctantly.

He brought down the plastic spatula one more time, and for the last time that day.

"Oww! Sorry, sorry, sorry, sir!"

"I know it seems so, but I hope you have learned your lesson, little one."

"Yes," she sniffed as she answered, "I have. I am very sorry, sir."

"Good girl." Scottie took her off his knee. "You go upstairs, little one. I'll make you some breakfast and do your tablet-ie thingies." Her word for those painkillers amused him. *Another simple thing that makes you so adorable,* he thought. He then continued, "And some more water as well. But you will keep those shorts around your ankles, unless, of course, they completely come off when you walk upstairs. Now, come here." Scottie pulled her towards him and gave her a big cuddle. One of his hands moved lower to rub her bottom.

Giving a satisfied sigh, still shedding a few tears she gave a tight hug and smiled. "I do love you."

"I know, little one," Scottie smiled

"Oh, you do, do you. Maybe I should take it back, shall I?" not expect that response.

"Do you want to go back over my knee, little girl?"

Heather shook her head, "No, sir."

"Then behave, and don't you ever threaten that, or I will

seriously give you a damn good hiding, I better be making myself clear." Scottie words were soft yet firm.

She realised her behaviour had gone a little too far... again. "Yes, sir. You do. I was only joking. Sorry, sir."

"Good girl. I forgive your naughtiness. I was gonna continue and say *I love you, too*. I'll do so now. I love you, too, little one." He kissed her forehead. "Now head upstairs. I'll be up in a few minutes. I'll also take you across my knee, but this time to rub some cream into you bottom. Be a nice way to start the day."

"Thank you, sir. For that... and the spanking. I did need it. Dealing with my behaviour was a good way to start the day. Rubbing cream into my poor bottom is a bonus." Heather had stopped crying, but remained teary eyed. It became with happiness as well as the pain she felt across her bottom. She wiped the tears from her eyes and gave Scottie a big kiss, turned and shuffled her way upstairs, her shorts still around her ankles.

It had taken nearly a week for Heather's bottom to heal fully. This was not a problem for Scottie since it was enjoyable to take her across his knee and apply cream in such bountiful amounts.

With good timing, Heather's bottom healed in time for a camping trip with her friends. Taking the week off work was fun, but being away from Scottie was a snag in her plans.

They would send each other a goodnight text every night, knowing it would be worthwhile spending a week apart; after all, the reunion would be highly enjoyable.

After a week of camping, Heather was naturally happy to see Scottie again. Work was a different story. After enjoying herself all week, it was a strain to take any pleasure *in work. **Her moodiness became noticeable.***

Scottie allowed a few days of Heather's moodiness at work to go as if unnoticed, figuring it would take a few days for her to settle back into a normal working routine.

This did not occur.

Since they took their breaks together, he decided he would wait no longer to *discuss* her behaviour. This he would do in the staff room.

He timed it well so that they took their break when no one else was. This would present itself with the perfect opportunity to deal with the situation.

There was a door to walk through that leads to the staff room. Nobody would hear him dealing with his moody little girlfriend. If he took a stool and sat near the door, which needed to be pushed in order to enter, there would not be much of a problem.

"What's wrong, little one?" Scottie took the stool, moved it towards the door, and sat down.

"Work. Just not in the mood." Heather said as she slumped into the settee. "Why are you sitting over there blocking the door? Are you guarding me from monsters? Aw, how sweet. I'd kiss you if I could be bothered to get up," she giggled. "How about that. First time I've smiled at work today. Well, apart from when I got a glimpse of you-Noooo." She suddenly realised something with shock horror.

"Yes, little one. You need motivating. And I so know a simple solution in solving this sitch. Damn, that was a mouthful," he realised, shaking his head. "Anyway... come here, please."

"Nooo... You can't." Heather looked around to see if there was anything to hold on to in case Scottie attempted to lift or pull her. *Oh, for the love of mighty* Hmph! *Typical, there's not.*

"Don't worry, I've got it covered. No one can hear us beyond that other door. If someone enters, we'll hear them. It will then allow me to lean back and make sure no one can get in. I'll tell them you've got your zippier stuck." He laughed at such a lame excuse. "Excuse me. This is no laughing matter."

"No, you won't." Heather had made up her mind.

"Just kidding, little one. You don't even have a zippier." Scottie laughed; halfway through, he became very serious, "Anyway, you need a spanking. Frankly, that's just what you'll get. I'll say you're just tucking yourself in, that you'll be no more than a minute. At that point, you can pull up your pants... voilà. So come here, right now."

Heather knew it was pointless to argue. She did as he told her. Within a few seconds, she stood by his right side. "If you're going to spank me, right here and now, don't expect me to pull down my own pants," she let him know in a brat-filled tone.

He grinned, amused. "Of course." Scottie loosened Heathers belt. Not that there was a need to nor had she done so purposely, but Heather recently had lost a little weight. Because she was wearing loose fitting trousers, they fell to her feet without the need to unbutton them.

"You will bend over my knee yourself, little girl, and don't you dare give me any backchat." Scottie allowed her to keep her panties up, wanting the pleasure of peeling them down while she was over his knee.

"Yes, sir." Heather gently leaned on his legs and positioned herself over his lap.

Slowly, Scottie peeled down her panties. "A beautiful, beautiful bottom. One that has been very naughty."

Knowing he had no time to waste, he started to spank, making sure his hand landed hard, but keeping the pace slow, so that he could hear the door if someone were to walk through.

"You will not be working with such an attitude, my girl. If you wish a change in career, by all means, speak with me. That way, if there is anything I can do, I can help you in anyway possible. For now, little one, when I am finished, I better see your mood improve," he scolded.

"But it's work-Ow! Sorry, sir." Heather felt him beginning to spank much harder now. She decided to remain quiet and not attract any more attention than the sound of a hand smacking bare flesh.

Remaining silent himself, hearing for the door, he spanked for the next minute or so in silence. It proved to be a wise move. He heard the door. Immediately he stopped. Heather looked so damn cute with a pink bottom and a look of panic etched on her face as she turned to look at Scottie for direction.

She froze.

Someone attempted to open the staff room door, but Scottie had leaned back to prevent anyone from entering. "One sec. Heather's tucking herself in. Only be a minute."

"Dude? You are a *dude*, man! Almost better than me." It was the Maestro.

"No, it's not like that," Scottie said, laughing, very much relieved it was the Maestro that had nearly caught them in the middle of a spanking. "She'll be done in a minute… or so."

"Hey, say no more. I'll take some fresh air. But mate, your duplicitous attempts are seriously wanting; your casual loquaciousness is not so convincing." The Maestro roared with laughter. "Hey! I can't see through doors, but I know that look. I purchased some rhyme of the day bog-roll. But still, mate, leave ya' to it. Sweeet!"

The Maestro's laughter faded.

Although they both heard the door close, Scottie wanted to check that the coast was clear. This he would do after recovering from the shock of someone nearly catching them in the act... along with the Maestro's vocabulary.

He gazed down upon Heather, who remained frozen over his knee. At that point, even if she wanted to, she was unable to make a sound. He managed to slip out his phone from his pocket.

He quickly wrote a text: Corner now. Keep pants down.

"Uh-huh," she responded, only just, as Scottie showed her the message. She did as he told her, rising off his lap and shuffling along to the corner as fast as she could considering her pants and panties were around her ankles.

Scottie peeked out of the door and checked to see if anyone was there. He quickly checked the other door, and as he had hoped, the coast was clear. He went back and sat in the same position. "Back. It's safe."

She turned around and expressed shock with this second interruption from the same man. "What is it with Franklin interrupting my spankings? What timing is that?"

"It is strange. Anyhow, come here again, little one. Over my knee. We may not have much time left to do this." Scottie knew they were both fortunate that the Maestro... or *The* Maestro, as Franklin preferred it, discovered them. *It really was a pretty lame excuse. Still... it would be a case of* prove it. *Not that anyone is likely to make a big thing of it all. Then again, it's not so bad an excuse... I'll say 'I'm tucking myself in. I'm sure no one needs to see anything here',* he thought, amused at his comical excuse... *Wait a sec. Did you? You better not be shaking your head, little girl.*

Heather shook her head. "No... I can't." She began to pull up her panties and pants.

In a very stern manner, Scottie scolded, "You drop those

right now, little girl! I am not joking around here. You will drop your pants, come here and bend over my knee or I will use that hard plastic spatula. I better be making myself clear!"

"No, No!" Heather let go of her pants and pulled down her panties. She walked fast towards Scottie and bent over his lap.

"I will spank you twelve times, little girl. And you will count them. Forget, and we will start over again."

"What? Ow-1! ... 2! ... 3! ... 4! ..." Heather continued to count, frozen just like before. She looked so cute, almost like a deer caught in headlights. Instead, it was a little brat and her spanked bare bottom caught over her boyfriend's lap. She was dreading the thought of someone bursting through the door or, even just as worse, overhearing, "...8! ... 9! ... 10-Ouch! ... 1-Ooh! ... 12-Ow! Thank you, sir. Sorry, sir. May I please get up now?"

"Yes, little one, you can." Rubbing her bottom, he tapped it.

Heather stood and pulled up her pants and panties as fast as she could. They sat on the settee and cuddled for a minute before spending the remainder of their lunch break outside where they spoke about the spanking.

Although reluctant, Heather found it highly exciting. As exciting as it was, she had no desire to rush into being so naughty at work again for fear of a repeat. She promised to be good.

This may be easier said than done, she thought.

She felt a lot happier at work with a spanked bottom. Though as for behaving, all she could do was try her best. *Try* being the operative word.

Um, eep! she realised.

Before heading back to work, something Scottie said had dawned on her. "Did you say I was tucking myself in?"

"Er, yeah. Well, at least, I think so... Oh." Scottie realised, fairly amused.

"Yes, *Oh*." In contrast, Heather was not so amused. "I don't tuck in this blouse."

"Not to worry. He'll think we were doing something else. Not spanking." Scottie waved his hand, dismissing any worry.

"I don't want him thinking... *anything!*" she responded.

Scottie laughed, looking at his cute little girlfriend with amazement. "He already does, I'm sure. You are aware of what you look like? Besides, I'll tell him I meant that *I* was tucking *myself* in, not you. He won't believe me, but still."

Heather rolled her eyes at his compliment, but admitted, "It's not so bad, I suppose."

"See you soon, little one," Scottie said as he kissed Heather.

They both made their way back to their respective office areas.

What Heather had not realised was that her punishment was not over. *Not just yet... my ever so cute, naughty little thing,* Scottie thought.

Two hours after their lunch break, she received a text message: Did u fink ur punishment was over? I dint av time 2 give u a propa spanking. I will fin it wen we get ome. N yes it will b wit da plastic spatula. Only 12 more 2 go. Behave little one. Stay cute. Love you xxxx

As Scottie expected, there was no response. It did not matter. He could imagine the look on Heather's face when she read the text message.

Of interest

*T*he list below is of historical events, films, music, etc. mentioned in this book, which might be of interest to the reader.

Historical events:

- Wars of the Roses (1455-1487 ~ Three main areas of conflict: 1455-1464; 1469-1471; 1483-1487)
- Second World War (1939-1945)
- Vietnam War – *Second Indo-China War* (1959-1975)

Films:

- Back To The Future trilogy (1985, 1989, 1990)
- Shrek (2001 - and its subsequent sequels)
- Austin Powers (1997 - and its subsequent sequels)
- Euro Trip (2004)

Music:

- Get Outta My Dreams, Get into My Car – Billy Ocean (1988)
- Scottie Doesn't Know – Lustra (2004)

Football:

- Estonia (0) v (3) England: Wednesday, 6 June 2007

Spank to the future...

During 2007, with some alterations early in the following year, *R.S. Tanner* penned the short spanking stories within this book; along with the Spring of 2008, *Taming Of The Brat: M/F Spanking Stories (Volume One)** is published.

This is his first book, and if you have become a fan of his work [thank you... and might I say just how lucky you are, too ;)], you should keep a weather eye out for further books by the same author. Such works in progress are *A Spank In Time: M/F Spanking Stories (Volume Two)** and *A Brat By Any Other Name...: An M/F Spanking Novel.*

There are plans by the author to write many more spanking books. When his non-spanko activities and projects [or when not spanking a little brat] allow him time, he looks forward to writing those as well.

---

* In regards as to why the short stories books have a volume number, there are certain stories that have sequels planned.

[I have noticed that, technically speaking, the *M/F* part of the sub-title is not entirely accurate; one story within this book is M/FF; another is M/FFF. My intention is more to separate it from other themes, such as F/F; F/M; or M/M... not that anyone is likely to begin a semantic debate]

                    Happy Spanking ;)
                    R.S. Tanner

www.ingramcontent.com/pod-product-compliance
Ingram Content Group UK Ltd.
Pitfield, Milton Keynes, MK11 3LW, UK
UKHW041257180426
11947UKWH00008B/528